but now am found

but now am found

PATRICIA HORVATH

www.blacklawrence.com

Executive Editor: Diane Goettel
Cover Design: Jeffrey LeBlanc
Cover Art: Jeffrey LeBlanc
Book Design: Amy Freels

Published 2023 by Black Lawrence Press.
Printed in the United States.

For Jeff

Contents

Wakey Nights

Fifteen across, five letters: Night in Nicaragua. She wrote *noche,* she wrote it in pen. Do the easy ones first.

Her coffee had turned cold, dregs of the pot. Behind her eyes a steady thrum. She squinted, blurring words, rubbed her eyes with chafed knuckles.

Twenty-one across, seven letters: Site of Triangle. Do the easy ones first because it was important to be methodical. She smoked in this way, lighting each new cigarette at half-hour intervals, five cigarettes so far.

Bermuda, where planes went down. She filled in the letters, all caps.

She did not know why she'd wakened so early, sitting up in bed, hugging her knees, telling herself it was nothing, this headache, a mother's low anxiety. Silly to bundle into her robe, grope her way down the hall to her daughter's room where the bed was untouched, sheets taut, hospital-like in their precision. She pulled back the comforter as though perhaps. Foolish, she said aloud. A broken curfew, that was all, she should be angry.

For a while she'd played Solitaire, spreading cards on the kitchen table, listening to the oldies station. But the cards were alarming—suicide king, ace of spades, that jack with the axe at his head. Why depict them that way? And the crackle of words on the radio. Happy Meal, Proof of Purchase, Drive By, State Lines. In her rush to switch it off, she'd upset the ashtray, spilling butts onto the floor.

The cigarettes were her daughter's. She'd found them, two unopened packs, hidden in the girl's bureau. Two packs of Kools, five condoms in garish red wrappers, blue eye shadow, drugstore perfume. She hadn't known about the cigarettes, nor the condoms, certainly not those. So there were boys—no, a boy—someone hunched in a leather jacket, mumbling, or earnest perhaps, with short hair and a football sweater. Could this be right? What were they like now, boys? And what else didn't she know? Scribbling notes on yellow Post Its: *Do the laundry, do your homework, there's casserole for the microwave, Love*. Hefting patients twice her weight to get at bedpans, prodding for veins, rubbing lotion into torsos, reaching to change glucose bags, untangling wires, retying gowns until her arms ached and her feet swelled in the white shoes she kicked off the moment she got home each night, her daughter already asleep or maybe, she thought now, pretending. Because what did she really know?

Sixteen and sneaky-quiet, whip thin. A temper that could wear anyone down. Wailing, *Why, why can't I ever have the car, what's the point in my even getting a license?*

Suspect, victim, barricade, police sketch, until she'd turned the damned thing off, knocking ashes to the floor.

Danger, she knew, was everywhere. No need to leave home. Candles sparked blazes, stoves leaked gas, animals turned rabid, even food concealed toxins. Still, one could take heed. Seal cracks, lock doors, read labels. One could control things indoors.

You keep that cell phone on, she'd warned. *But ma, the movies, c'mon!* And now it rang, uselessly.

Fourteen down: Father of Rome. She knew that one. She had to think.

The sun was beginning to rise, dim shapes taking form in her neighbor's yard—swing set, sandbox, hedges. Somewhere a penned up dog was trying to bark itself free. The geraniums shivered in their boxes, a sudden wind scattering dead leaves across the empty driveway. *Make sure you're home by midnight and—I mean it—you leave that phone on.*

But she'd never listened, not through years of piled up words: *Now I Lay Me, Drink Your Milk, Don't Wiggle That Tooth, Clean Your Room, Put It Under The Pillow, Look Both Ways, I Don't Care What The Other Kids, Once A Month Yes I Know, Don't Talk Back, Two For Cramps, Take An Umbrella, Keep Your Phone On, Twelve O'clock, Period.*
Years of words. Reprimands, sweetness. Honey and baby and bun. *Honey bun, baby cakes, I could eat you, gobble gobble.* Blowing air into a tiny navel, the girl wriggling, shrieking, kicking fat legs in delight. Then—later—*Ma, don't call me that why can't you just use my name?* Summer days, strawberries rinsed from the hose, her daughter running naked through the sprinkler, not caring who might see. Or blizzards, the house swaddled in snow, a perfect, muffled world. Just the two of them, the way she'd planned it, right from the start. *You and me, pal.* Popcorn, Old Maid, anatomy texts piled on the table, studying late into the night so she could pass the exam, earn her pin, take care of them always. *You and me, who needs anyone else?*

If she could sleep. Lose herself in the murky world, wake to brightness. Her daughter eating breakfast, rumpled and defensive with some last-second excuse. Her own relief calcifying to anger. "Wakey nights" she called these sleepless hours. Wakey nights cooing the girl through some babyhood terror. Singing Mister Sandman, telling her about his castle of sand with its sandy furniture and turrets and moat and *Yes, I'll build one for us, a castle with a drawbridge; we'll live there someday.*

On the page, order and sense. Father of Rome, seven letters. There were two, though, twin infants with their sucking mouths. Romulus, Remus, abandoned to die but for the wolf.

A car pulled into the driveway. A car! Not hers. Two men in trench coats stepped from a dark green sedan.

Abandoned, but why? And what had happened to the wolf?

The men conferred by the hood of the car. One of them pointed.

The puzzle was filling too quickly. She needed to slow down. She needed coffee, fresh coffee, to quell the pounding in her head. It was louder now, it competed with the knocking on the door.

Two men in trench coats, they could not come in.

Ma'am, she heard. *Ma'am, please.*

But it was only grief that would find her, grief on the other side of the door, banging, insistent, and what was another word for that?

Sea Change

She listens.

A conch to her ear, she hears the ocean's faint roar. Hours since he stormed off. She's tucked in the children, listened to their prayers. She's cleared the table scraps, swept sand from the cottage, changed the muddied water in the pail by the screen door, brought in their towels, scratchy with wind and sun. The conch is worn smooth, an oceanic telephone. She puts it back on its shelf, walks out to the deck, lowers herself into a sagging canvas chair. Her girth an amazement, slowing her down. The sea churns, choppy with swells, a breeze lifting the small hairs that have escaped her braid. Tomorrow or the next day it will storm. She shivers in her shift, her legs and feet bare. The baby writhes and turns, sloshing in its salty sea. She puts a hand to her swollen belly, listens for the sound of tires raking pebbles on the road.

A drink, he'd said, I'm going for a drink. Slamming the screen door behind him. Stupid their quarrel, she regrets it now. Because what's a day, really? And so what if he wants to cut the week short, avoid the Sunday traffic? Have a day to relax before returning to his two-packs-of-Tums-a-week job? Was it, he'd said, too much to ask? But the fireworks, the children had wailed, we'll miss the fireworks! And then, of course, there was the heat, the stifling city heat; did he have any idea what that was like in her condition?

Easy enough for her, he'd replied, relaxing here while he toiled away.

Relaxing, ha! Shows how little he knew. Trapped in this cottage, day after day of rain. The children bored, bickering. Endless games of Rummy and War, soggy peanut butter and jelly sandwiches. Damp towels, mildewed paperbacks, swollen window sashes, cereal and crackers going stale overnight.

True, they'd had their sunny days, a walk into town for Italian ices and rides on the merry-go-round. Afternoons building castles, digging in low tide for fat white worms. But what she wouldn't give for a little peace. To come home from work, mix a drink, watch a movie. Or go to dinner with friends. Something anyway. All the things he took for granted. And then when he came here, for his week at the shore...

One week, he interrupted. One lousy week...

Yes, yes, she knew. How hard he worked, all of that. But what about her? While he was lying on a towel, listening to some game on the radio. Drinking beer with the other vacationing fathers. Or flying kites with the boy, leaving the girl to play alone by the water, the tide coming in, up to her waist already, my God, she couldn't be everywhere at once, could she? Especially now, worn out and expecting.

And did she always have to be so God damned melodramatic? That's what he wanted to know. As if the girl were in danger, as if he'd let that happen. He was going for a drink!

For hours she's been expecting him. Their last night of vacation, a shame. He should be with her, in this low-slung empty chair. Listening to the sea, running through their list of baby names, his choices, hers, wondering how this new little creature might be stamped, eyes and mouth, which of them it might turn out to resemble. She is anxious to see it, the baby. Anxious for him to come home.

She takes up her knitting, the booties she'd abandoned, though she feels no desire to knit. She might, she thinks, make a cup of tea. Or start a new jigsaw puzzle. Something to distract her from what she knows she's about to do, though she's sworn she would not, even as she dials the number. Noise in the background—laughter, music, shouting. His voice slurry with alcohol. Did he have any idea how late it was?

All right, all right. His last night of vacation. Just one more, the bartender was bringing it over. Then he'd come straight home.

He hangs up without saying good-bye. And didn't that just beat all? Sloshed, after he'd insisted on taking the car, after she'd asked him not to. A short walk, would've done him good. Well, he was in no condition to drive, short trip or no. Another drink and one more for the road, she knows how he gets when he gets going. If he wants to stay, fine, just hand over the keys.

She straps on a pair of worn white sandals, locks both the doors. The children, she thinks, will be fine.

At the end of the line of cottages she has to stop. The baby is kicking. She presses her knuckles to the small of her back, the pain knotted there. The first contraction washes over her. She breathes, surfaces. Sees moon, cottages, seawall—familiar things. Closer now to the bar than to home, she turns onto the access road. The wind has picked up, a hint of fall in the air. Waves break against the shore, a soothing sound. Late at night, when she can't sleep, it comforts her.

The road is dark; she takes her time. Soon she can see headlights coming from the parking lot. She knows this place, of course, has been here before, and to places like it, The Rusty Scupper, The Lobster Trap, The Salty Dog, places with ships' wheels on the wall, fishermen's nets hung from ceilings, a dartboard, a jukebox, Golden Oldies from when she was the age of these tanned and muscled boys, these girls in cutoffs and halter tops, townies who know they won't be carded, who can drink all night because they won't wake hung over, not even faced with a day of mowing lawns, serving soft ice cream, or babysitting a pack of whiny children, just as she had done, years ago, while she waited for something to happen.

Her husband is at a table, his back to her. His hand grips the hand of a man half his age, a boy really, a good looking boy with floppy, sun-lightened hair. A ring of spectators eggs them on. The boy grimaces. His hand is locked in her husband's hand, their forearms pressed together. Then the boy's arm yields, a cheer erupts, and her husband is downing the victory shot that someone, a girl, has passed to him. He does not turn around, does not see her, but she knows how he must look, his broad and handsome face flushed with triumph, his rakish grin. She wants to reach out, tousle his hair. The girl, all cleavage, leans forward, her chest in his face. She pours him a beer. In one quick motion his puts his arm around her waist and pulls the girl, squealing, onto his lap.

She does not think. The second contraction nearly knocks her down. Hey, someone says, hey, you all right? and he is turning in his chair, still holding the girl, even as she reaches for the pitcher. Beer gushes over his head, down his back, onto the floor. The girl shrieks. Who is this woman, this crazed and hugely pregnant woman, and why is she causing this commotion? He jumps up, grabs her from behind. That's when she feels it, her water break, fluid coursing down her legs, soaking her sandals. The front of her shift is drenched. Beer drips from his hair, his beard. She is slipping in the muck, clinging to him for support. Hang on, he says, hang on, but she is losing her grip, no way to stop what has begun, the tide inside her, the baby on its way now, too early and far too late.

But Now Am Found

Metal

The brace encased her, chin to hip, hard plastic and metal. She wore it for her spine, that snaky column, a second body to reshape the damaged one. Winter the metal at her neck was cold, filmy with fingerprints; summer it was too hot for him to touch. She hid it with turtlenecks, smocks, silky scarves. Her shoes big and clunky—*for support*, she said. At movies, at meals, under glass-shaded lamps in the library where they studied, she sat upright, unable to bend. Wispy hair fell into her face whenever she leaned forward. His own hair nearly as long—*Like Jesus.* She said it to tease him, and in retort he called her Teacher's Pet, extending the phrase, hard on the "r." Good girl, ambitious girl, yearbook editor, chorus soprano, player of bright riffs on her parents' secondhand piano. So different from his slacker habits, classes skipped, joints smoked beneath the bleachers at lunch. The activities kept her parents off her back, she said, and she'd knock on her metal torso. It was what he loved about her—the breeziness, her confidence despite it all.

The brace was until she stopped growing and some extra time to be safe. How long precisely, who could say? Every three months she went for check ups.

He tried to imagine what it was like for her. The weight of the brace lifting from her hips. The paper gown, the x-ray machine, her spine illuminated on the light table. The doctor's finger tracing wayward vertebrae. His veined hands, hairy at the knuckles.

The day he saw the swan he knew he would buy it for her. A silver swan, its chain clipped to the velvet-backed tray in the mall's jewelry cart. One eye in silhouette: tourmaline, beryl, malachite, jade, chemical words recalled from Earth Science class, fancy words for green. There were other things he thought she might like: silver hoops tiny enough not to bang against the brace, a circular broach, but the swan was special, sprung from ugliness, then look! Like the beauty he saw in her, locked away. A month of yard work the necklace cost, four consecutive Saturdays spent raking dead leaves into plastic bags, but what was that? Their anniversary nearly here, a year from the day she'd agreed to meet him at the movies, and it was at the movies that he handed her the wrapped box, waiting until the lights rose and the theater began to fill for the next show.

The way she looked at him, so seriously, mouth turned down as if in disapproval, for a moment he was afraid he'd done wrong. She lifted the swan from its cotton bed, let it dangle between them, its eye a cold green speck. Not real emerald, he explained, but the silver, that's real. She smiled, touched a knuckle to her eye. Was she crying? The theatre was so dim. He wiped his glasses on his shirttail. It's lovely, she said, help me with it.

He had trouble threading the chain beneath the metal at her neck, attaching the clasp. The necklace did not hang quite right, the swan nearly concealed by a crossbar of some sort. But they both knew it was there and that was what mattered, she said.

His second gift, a month later, was almost better, the driver's license they'd been waiting for. With this came a shift in his status, her parents expecting to meet this boy who would take their daughter out, drive her places in his parents' car.

Because he was nervous he smoked a joint on the way over, just a hit to calm him so that later, sitting on one of the matching floral armchairs in her living room, chatting with her mother about the courses he was taking (Algebra I, Intermediate Spanish, Biology, Civics, nothing special, nothing AP, homeroom their one period in common) he hoped the gum masked his breath. A white crucifix hung behind the couch, Jesus caked in plastic blood. The only other artwork a painting of an ocean at sunset...or was it sunrise? Wondering this made him want to laugh; he shouldn't have smoked. Her upright piano was against one wall, but not a book in sight; how did she get so smart? Her mother's face a crumpled bag, blonde hair gone to rust. She wore an apron, offered sugar cookies and pink lemonade, warnings about speed limits and curfew. The movies, Mom, her daughter groaned. We're only going to the movies.

Her father he saw briefly and just that once. A big squared off man with meaty hands. When they shook hello he felt the man's high school ring, a gaudy thing, gumball sized. His grip too hard. If there's trouble, he said, leaving the sentence unfinished. Other times he heard the man banging away in the basement, hammers pounding, drills boring holes.

He thought it would change things, being able to drive, spending time alone with her, but it didn't seem to much. At the movies they still shared tubs of popcorn, scrabbling through kernels until she shushed him, then holding hands through the rest of the show. Always during the week she was busy but sometimes he'd sit with her in the library and pretend to study while she worked. Once he took her to the beach, parking as far as possible from the other cars—couples in back seats, boys doing donuts, their tires screeching on ice. He kept the radio low so it didn't matter what song was sung, the vocals a backdrop to soothe or excite. The heat was cranked high and they took off their coats and sweaters. She loosened his ponytail from its rubber band, smoothed the hair over his collar. He loved how her hair smelled of lemon and pine. With her he could imagine himself someone ambitious, an A student, scholarship material, someone to make parents proud.

He reached across the driver's seat, pulled her towards him, awkward in the tight space, her brace making it even more difficult. They had kissed before, of course, in the dark of the movies or briefly before saying goodnight. Not like this though, with his arms around her, the windows fogging and the squeal of tires growing faint. He stroked the coarse wool of her shirt—an arm, a shoulder—inching his way towards her breast, touching instead something foreign—a buckle, a strap—that made him recoil.

I know, she said. It's in the way.

No... it's all right... it's just...

The thing you don't expect, was what he wanted to say. Hardness where softness should be. Metal for flesh, a thing with no give.

Uncertain what to do, he kissed her again, lightly, ignoring what was between them until he forgot it altogether and they nearly missed her curfew.

A Sunday, she told him she'd faked cramps. He biked across town, concerned because it wasn't like her to lie. What with the sermon, the hymns, the jelly donut social, her parents would be gone for hours. Still she'd urged him to hurry.

No one answered the door, so he let himself in. Her shades were drawn, the room dark to hide that she'd been crying. Something about a grandmother. She sobbed, barely coherent. Her grandmother down south, mobs of cousins she barely knew. Floppy-eared, living in shacks. The way she described it—cows to milk, chickens pecking worms. *The middle of freakin' nowhere. All July and August. It isn't fair!*

He would forget about her.

No he would not. She had to believe him.

She stomped her foot. The stupidity of it. And what she did next astonished him, pulling her shirt right over her head, throwing it to the floor.

Look at me! Look! As if things aren't crappy enough.

Ribs, clavicle, shoulder blades, he stared at her fragmented body. Flat breasts in a white cotton bra. Two bars attached to a molded corset, like a pair of metal suspenders. There were screws, bolts, springs, straps; how could she stand it?

She sat on the bed, almost as tall as him because the brace held her rigid. Her eyes red-rimmed, the lids puffed. If he could touch her, reach into that awful cage. Wait, she said. I want you to see. His stomach churned with excitement. She kicked her pants loose and stood up. A greasy leather strap locked the corset in place over white bikinis. Her arms were gooseflesh; what would her stomach look like? He could feel himself growing hard, wanting her.

Take it off, he whispered. Just this once.

I can't. I won't be able to get it back on.

I'll help.

You don't know how. It's tricky.

Show me.

He lifted her hair, loosened a screw at the base of her head. The metal neck ring slid apart. He locked it back in place.

See? What else?

I don't know.

Sssshhh . . . it'll be easy. You do this all the time.

Not alone.

But you're not alone.

He unbuckled the corset and the brace shifted, loose on her hips. He pried it apart. She did the rest, pushing it from her body, stepping out.

Without the brace's support, she leaned slightly to the right. Porcelain, he thought, meaning not her skin, which was pale from lack of sun, but the bones themselves, how fine they were, how easily he could imagine them shattering. He put his hand on her stomach, the slack muscles beneath making him nearly weak.

From the pocket of his jeans he removed a crumpled joint. Are you crazy, she said; it'll stink up the whole house. He ignored her, raising the shade to blow a long hit out the window then stubbing the joint on the sill. She was sitting on the bed, frowning, but not really angry he could tell. What did she want? He took off his glasses, his shirt. She kept on her underwear and the swan necklace that she always wore. They made a tent, holding each other beneath the covers, hiding from what would come next, her slack-jawed grandmother, the cousins in overalls; it couldn't be as bad as she said. He pressed himself against her, felt her breasts through the thin cotton of her bra, thinking he would be happy enough to die right there until she said we better stop.

The brace would not fit.

He'd managed the leather strap all right but the ring at the back of her head would not come together and when he tried to force it the brace's lower part pivoted, causing her to cry out. Oh shit oh shit oh shit she moaned and he tried taking it apart, starting from the top but the strap would not buckle and her parents would be back any minute, she'd think of something, she said, only he'd better go. He kissed her in a rush and biked fast all the way home.

Afterwards there was silence. Her phone privileges revoked. She's not allowed to talk, her mother said, you'd better stop calling. That stern woman with her apron and sugar, her mouth a jagged line.

He waited in homeroom, at the cafeteria table they shared; he went to the yearbook office, the music room. No one had seen her. At night he would ride past her house, the lights always off and her father's car missing from the driveway.

Fire

The post mark was smudged, the card showing a chapel, white and scabby against a bright sky. And the name, Salvation Valley, printed in red across the bottom.

You are on the forbidden list—can you believe such a thing?—but I found a way to sneak this out. Do not write back. Here they make us rise at dawn, the days being spent in chores and prayer. There are hikes, testi-monials, a beat up piano, out of tune. I tried to warn you. Love.

He fixed on that last word, one they'd never said. How to read it, how to understand. He pictured her scrubbing potatoes, hoeing weeds, hands raw, fingernails dirty and chipped. Always she'd kept them meticulous, the better to play. The piano would be battered, with yellowed keys, but it was something at least, some small conso-lation. At prayers she knelt on a splintered floor, slept in a barracks, he could see her turning and turning on her hard little cot, mosquito bitten, sweaty inside the brace. He would steal his father's car, rescue her. Go to her house and confront her parents. He finished the school year with Cs, mowed lawns, drove around aimlessly, the radio loud with songs of love's rise and fall.

Her letter, weeks later, was even more terse. *You are in my thoughts. Here they do not believe in deformity, it being a mark of sin.* In the accompanying photo she was lined up, second row, before the cha-pel. Everyone alike in khakis, baggy t-shirts that covered their collar bones. Still, it was clear she did not wear the brace. Her face was sun-burned, her eyes in a squint. *I have earned privileges, piano hymns dur-ing weekday service. So strange to find myself in this place. I'll try to write again. Take care.*

He thought about Moonies, Manson girls, Krishnas with their shaved heads, their robes the orange of prison uniforms. How long would it take?

So strange to find myself. Strange, indeed, his level-headed girl, too smart for tales of angels and clouds, devils with pitchforks, eternal flames. And that word, deformity. Surely she didn't believe such a thing. Because how could her body, her beautiful body which he'd seen and touched, be a mark of sin?

She was crooked was all. Stoop-shouldered, slightly leaning. With-out the brace she would become hunched, her ribs weighing on her heart, compressing it. She'd told him that. Had they seized it, locked it away? Tossed it in a bonfire like so much trouble? The week before, he'd had an eye exam and his prescription had been strengthened. Until the eye drops wore off he'd felt vulnerable, the world unfamiliar. In the photo she'd sent no one wore glasses.

Water

The carnival was coming.

All day men worked in the heat of the municipal lot assembling rides from pieces stashed in trailers. The Tilt-A-Whirl, the carousel and Scrambler, he watched them take shape. Games of chance appeared overnight, dartboards, mounted rifles, shelves of plastic-sheathed animals, sad-eyed dogs, benignly smiling lambs.

Late August, he'd not heard from her again. Had he imagined it, their time together, the grave look on her face when they kissed, the taste of cherry Chapstick and the way she'd grab his arm in the movies, her image distinct as ever then wavering, a mirage—he shook his head—a mirage in a sundress splayed with tiny blue flowers. She was in a group of girls, dowdy ones, some of whom he recognized. The carnival's opening night, he'd biked over hoping to meet friends. She smiled at his approach, excused herself from her gaping companions.

A week, she said, a week she'd been back.

You could've called.

They won't let me use the phone.

Or written.

It was…you don't know. It wasn't like I could just walk to a mailbox.

What was it like then?

Gently he put his hands on her shoulders, claiming her. She kept still, her arms at her sides, her gaze focused on some distant point. She was shorter than he remembered. Her hair, sun bleached and brittle, was clipped back in a way that made her look severe. At her neck a plain gold cross. He toyed with it, rubbed it between his fingers. Who had given it to her?

You don't wear it anymore, he said.

The brace? I told you. I don't have to.

It was not what he meant and he suspected she knew that. He took her hand—briefly she let him—surprised at how soft it was, how tentative her grip. Side by side they walked down the Midway, nodding at acquaintances, answering each other's light questions— his summer was fine, boring really, she'd be back at school, yes, a full schedule. Colored lights flashed, music blared, the air reeked of burnt sugar and grease, molecules refusing to rest in the makeshift, buzzing world. He bought a cotton candy, their lips turning sticky from the treat and it was all he could to do to keep from kissing her right there on the Midway with everyone to see.

On the Tilt-A-Whirl they pressed their backs to the wall, struggling not to slide to the pit below. The Scrambler felt as if it might just fly apart—one loose nut or bolt to send them careening out to sea. She was thrown against his shoulder then propelled back. All around them were shrieks of mock terror and delight.

They played a game of chance.

He would win something—a kewpie doll, a coin purse, a string of beads; she could count on him. He placed a folded dollar on six, his lucky number, his birth month and date. The barker spun a wheel and the numbers blurred then slowed, ticking past the apex. He tried again, another folded bill. Each mark on the wheel denoted not a number but an ordinary moment from a life barely begun; he imagined them that way. The wheel stopped and he was an old man asleep in rumpled pajamas. Again and he was a baby, screaming for suck. Once more, he saw himself stroking a woman's dark hair as she bent over something. A flower bed? A fussing child? Beneath her thin shirt he could see the perfect knobs of her vertebrae.

They walked away empty-handed.

But there was nothing I wanted, she said. Nothing at all.

At the top of the Ferris wheel their car swayed, pinpricks of lights beneath their feet and the sulfurous whiff of low tide on the breeze. He could just glimpse the sea, a blaze where the sun was low. The mythical place where the earth fell away, where dragons appeared on old maps, a place he could take her where they could be out of reach. Win or lose, he had to try his luck, up in the air, finally alone, no one to see how she turned her face from his or hear her gentle no.

No. It's different now.

Different how? We're the same as before.

We're not. She'd folded her hands in her lap and she spoke as if to them. I've been born again. You haven't.

Born again? You don't believe that cartoon shit, do you?

She did not reply. The car began its slow descent. She leaned away from him, serene and aloof, slightly off center. It would get worse, this leaning. Year by year her spine would twist, ribs shifting, pressing the life from her heart. He understood that, even if she did not.

During his eye exam, when he'd looked into the optometrist's machine, the world had gone briefly sharp. Better? the doctor had asked. Fuzzy or clear? For a moment he could see each letter on the chart. Then something clicked, the lenses changed, and the world became indistinct again.

He could not hate her.

Their car had stopped. He thought about chance, the barker's spinning wheel, so much life still to go. He looked at her and felt nothing. He looked out towards the water and saw water.

Luck Was A Taxi

Trace minerals, you'll like it. Good and crisp.

He had not asked—the wine, the place, his pick. Trace minerals... meaning? Iron? Flint? Wine as a thing to be mined. She ordered mussels; he chose stone crab then returned to his complaint (rant, perhaps, too strong a word): blood on a blade, unassailable evidence, what the hell had he been thinking, that dimwit, bleeding heart judge? And tomorrow the quick flight to a nowhere town, the deposition that would keep him cooped up all day.

A glorified desk job when you get right down to it, he said. You, at least you get out in the world with your swatches and silks and... what's it... soirées?

Moiré. A fabric. As you well know.

He smiled at this little joke, his gentle mocking of her profession, its frivolity—not that he'd ever used that word. But how could beauty survive, he'd once asked, without people like him to first make the world safe? Lock up the bad guys, throw away the key.

Still the real work, by which he meant the dangerous work, wasn't done by men like him, men in smart suits who were handed the cases other men solved, men whose suits were not at all smart and whose shoes were dull from what things you did not want to know. She'd heard all this before and stopped herself now from objecting: How can you say that? It takes brains, real brains, to do what you do!

His own suits were impeccably tailored—worsted wools, tweeds, herringbones, shirts starched, lapels notched, a Windsor knot at his

19

throat, a glint of cufflinks, the straight line of a pocket square. Geometry. Because it was important, he said, to be precise, to notice the things that others overlooked: appearances, tics, the cut of a suit, a grimace or grin, the expression one adopted under oath. How else to get an edge?

The mussels arrived—slick, sweet, a good contrast to the wine. He cracked his crab, a trace of brine darkening the silk of his tie. It would stain. Well into her second glass, she felt the sharpness of the room abate, harpoons and hooks and that giant stuffed marlin above the bar losing their slight power to alarm. It was warm in the room and the wine made her flush. She thought about blotting the stain on his tie but didn't want to embarrass him. Instead she sat back, listening to the blur of words from other tables, words she had no reason to heed.

He waved off dessert, after dinner drinks. His flight was early; he'd see her home, it wasn't far, then catch a cab uptown.

They walked a dimly lit terrain of warehouses and loading docks, the restaurant an outpost in a neighborhood still too remote to be trendy. Because she'd worn heels, she had to take two steps for each of his, their strides a bit out of synch. Yet she liked walking beside him, their bodies nearly touching, the way he cupped her elbow at curbs or offered his arm, and how, even in heels, she had to lift her chin to look at him.

Mid-block, he stopped.

There, across the street, that loft, did she see? She followed his finger, an imaginary line that led to . . . she squinted, taking it in. Thick at the window, a curtain of birds. Crayola-breasted, heavy-winged, they tapped the glass, gripped the sill with bony talons, stretched their necks, pecked at tail feathers—bluebirds, parrots, finches—was that right? Birds and their shadows flitting about a brightly lit room.

They should be nesting, sound asleep. She thought she knew that much about birds, that they were diurnal, probably thrown off kilter by all the lights. The birds wheeled towards a mass of tromp l'oeil clouds, pink-tinged on a vaulted blue ceiling.

Imagine, he said, though she did not have to. Pent up like that, it's a crime.

No doubt he was right. Instead of digging for twigs, rubber bands, bits of twine, whatever detritus the world might yield, they made their homes in hard cages, no sun to warm their feathers, or breezes to cool, no rains to puddle in nests—monsoons, hurricanes, predators, what have you—so easy to romanticize nature, though she knew he'd disagree. And what joy to wake in this safe haven, surrounded by birds, their jeweled bodies and jubilant song.

His hand on her shoulder interrupted her thoughts. He steered her towards a side street, quiet this time of night. At the far end, blocks away, were pubs and cafés, the promise of life on an otherwise desolate stretch. Trash night, they stayed close to the stoops, avoiding the mounds at the curb.

Who do you suppose lives there? she asked.

Oh, some old kook. A fairy in a velvet smoking jacket. Granny.

Granny?

You know, that old lady from the cartoon. The one with the umbrella and canary.

Tweety, blissful and plump; she pictured him swinging in his cage, singing in that nasal voice, bars of sunlight on the floor, the staccato bursts of his cries for help. She could hear the click of her heels on the sidewalk, feel the dampness in the air, the threat of rain, and she turned up her collar, catching peripherally a rustling in the bags, the dark shape that streaked past them, causing her to gasp.

What? he said. It's nothing. Just a cat. Look.

Crouched in an alley the cat watched them through hard yellow eyes. A bit of trash was snared on one of its long claws. The cat bared its teeth. With a graceful motion it raised its paw and bit down.

See? Just a cat having dinner.

His tone said how silly to be so afraid, her nervousness unfounded. He put his arm around her, shielding her from her own imagination.

In grade school the boys had brought earthworms to class, dropping them on the girls' desks just to hear the girls shriek. During gym they snapped the elastic waistbands of the girls' shorts whenever the coach wasn't looking. The girls rolled their eyes, a stupid game, but they were careful to stick together. In the locker room one summer, at the municipal pool, she'd heard noises at the hinged transom. Boys, shaky on each other's shoulders, faces pressed to chicken-wired glass; boys, their tongues out, moaning. She'd been naked and had scrabbled for a towel. After that she kept her damp suit on, waited to shower at home; all the girls did. And they'd grown out of it, the boys, just as the teachers had said they would, best to ignore them meanwhile, them and their silly pranks, what harm really, it was just what boys do.

　. . . More afraid of you than you are of them, he was saying, meaning worms or rats or spiders, meaning her girlish fears, inconsequential. Only, how would he know?

　A couple approached them, arguing; she caught a few low words— *just because you say so*—the woman's mouth moving, moving—lipstick, noise, gum. The avenue pulsed with neon, music blared from bars, couples laughed, boys jostled each other, a woman wheeled a sleeping baby, short-skirted girls shivered, pushing the season. They waited for a light to change, two people in the reassuring surge. She was nearly home—there the corner laundry, there the tree whose high branches skimmed her window making her feel as if she lived in an aerie, this tree—no, *elm*, he'd specified, *elm* because it was a rare thing, what with blight, not just any old tree, didn't she know? She had sensed his disapproval, however slim, at her lack of observation.

　By the door to her building they kissed, a quick peck turning to something longer, his hand at the small of her back, fingers splayed, pressing. The air felt heavy, static-charged, and the wind lifted the hair at her neck. He took a step back, glanced at his watch. Not so late, really, perhaps he'd come up after all, what did she think?

It was tempting. The nearness of him, the way his body seemed larger in her small bed, his musky smell and the sweetness of lying beside him as he slept. If, in fact, he slept. And if he did, there would be the tumult of morning, lights switched on, the rush of faucets, toilet, gulps of coffee, sour breath, hurried good-byes.

Your flight... she began, and he said yes, she was right, though she'd said next to nothing. An early flight, he should go, he'd call her in a day or two.

She put on the kettle, changed into a fleecy robe. The wind was picking up. Branches scratched the window. Elm, oak or maple, she did not care. Something had taken root to screen her, the tree already greening, its leaves so early this year.

She brought her tea to the living room, settled into the cushioned window seat. A small commotion below as the rain began, people scurrying for cover, arms above their heads, a quick unfurling of umbrellas, a man sheltering a woman, rain sweeping the sidewalk.

Something was clawing at her, some feeling she could not name. Go to a room, an office, a home. Study the angles, the light. She could fashion a space in which people saw not themselves but an ideal of themselves, an ideal crafted from texture and hue, the weave of a carpet, the glow of a lamp, the small details of her own home— glass doorknobs, silk throw pillows, claw-foot tub—details he'd failed to note. Her job depended on this, on seeing, no less than his.

The sky had turned milky and the trees shone black against it, the pavement dark with rain, a world in monochrome.

Once, not long ago, they'd left a party to find that the nighttime sky had gone white with snow. New Years, they'd been together for only a few weeks. Her high heels slipped on the pavement; they'd had to take it slow. A man turned the corner, blocking their path. His torso was huge, arms like Easter hams. Beyond him the street glimmered in perfect, snow globe silence. The man stood still before them. He looked her up and down, a hungry man in a leather jacket and biker boots. No words were spoken, no one moved. She had the

sense that everything was about to change, irrevocably, and then a
cab came gliding down the street, its Off Duty light on, but the
driver slowed in response to her waving and motioned them inside.

In the back seat he'd slid his hand beneath her skirt, told her how
hot she looked. It had excited him, this near confrontation. Shaken,
she moved away, pressed her cheek to the glass.

The rain was coming in hard. She shut the window, finished her
tea, drew a bath.

Later, stepping into water, she wondered whether he'd been
drenched or if he'd been lucky enough to make it home in time. Luck
was all it was: getting home before the rain, finding the right chair in
the secondhand shop, choosing the winning ticket, the right or wrong
flight. Luck was a taxi, that small yellow miracle that had saved them
from...what? Perhaps nothing at all.

It wouldn't last. And that was the feeling, the thing that gripped
her, that and nothing more. The feeling had to do with his faith in his
own good fortune, a thing that, despite the show complaints, he
could depend upon, believing he'd forged it himself. Not for him the
rabbit's foot, the penny, the salt. Fools' balm to ward off those fears
without name, fears that lacked substance and force. He knew better
than that.

Steam was rising from the water. She shut off the tap, rested her
head on the tub rim, and let herself sink into the slowly cooling bath.

Never Let Go

I was thirteen, he was forty, give or take, and we were going on a date.

Get changed, my mother said. Roy's taking you out.

As far as I could tell Roy didn't go out. As far as I could tell Roy never went anywhere except his apartment, our house, and the restaurant where he tended bar. It wasn't anyone's birthday either.

Where's he taking us?

Not us, you. Wear something nice.

This was not a good idea; how could it be? My mother had only been seeing Roy for a few months but already I had compiled a list of crimes, crimes that I wrote in red Flair pen at night when I unlocked my diary.

1. He drinks. Budweiser, Captain Morgan, Cutty Sark.
2. Uses his empty glass as an ashtray.
3. Leaves his ashtray drinks lying around for me to pick up.
4. Has a tattoo of a mermaid and another of a hula girl.
5. Makes rules: Do the dishes, Clean your room, Take out the trash, Set the table, like it's his home.
6. Says you don't have one, that's the problem whenever I say You are not my father.
7. Chews with his mouth open—it's disgusting.

To be fair I also kept a list in blue Flair pen of what I called Good Points, which were two:

1. He has a red Cadillac convertible.

2. He has a monkey.

But (and now we're back to the other list)

8. He might get rid of the monkey because my mother says so.

They argued about this. It had to do with Roy maybe moving in and my mother saying things like Over my dead body if you think I'm living with some planet of the God damned ape. But Ranger wasn't an ape, just a little gray monkey in a diaper. I'd seen him once. My mother had stopped by Roy's apartment for some reason or another and there was Ranger jumping on a futon couch. He ran towards us, jibbering, mouth full of crooked yellow teeth. I stepped behind my mother. Roy, she screamed, Roy for Chrissakes, and Roy scooped Ranger into his arms.

He's just saying hello to the beautiful ladies, is all. Do you want to pet him, Sweetheart?

I did, but I was afraid. Afraid of what those monkey teeth might do. I stroked Ranger on the head. If we got to know each other, I was thinking, if he got used to me, it could be like having a little brother.

Aside from the futon couch, the only furniture in Roy's apartment was a table and two folding chairs. Roy, still holding Ranger, took a jug of wine from the fridge and filled two mugs. He poured me a glass of rusty looking water. The bottoms of his tattoos—fish tail, hula girl feet—peeked out from under the sleeves of his t-shirt. Ranger fidgeted, tugging at his diaper. I thought maybe I could train him to sit on my lap and eat bananas.

What does he eat? I asked Roy.

Whatever he can.

He thought that was funny. He started to laugh, Ranger bouncing on his knee, then he, Ranger, made this screeching sound and Roy yelled Oh shit just as my mother and I were covering up our noses because Ranger had let loose and it was worse, this monkey mess, than whatever you might imagine. I picked up the small can of air freshener from the table and the next thing I knew we were out in the cold, Roy holding Ranger, all of us choking and wheezing and crying because the air freshener turned out to be mace. What the hell, my mother asked, coughing her words, What the hell did you do that for?

I did not want to go on the date.

All right, she said. Get moving.

I swapped jeans for cords, sneakers for boots, sweatshirt for sweater. My mother said Jesus, you *could* put on a dress and Roy said Never mind, she's fine.

Roy's friend Lucky was in the living room drinking a can of Budweiser. As usual he wore a college sweatshirt beneath his tweed blazer, this time a dark blue one that said Smith. His cheeks were stubbly, his eyes bloodshot.

Princess, he said, rising from the couch. Your chariot awaits.

Lucky's driving us to the station, Roy said. He'd put on a suit and had flattened his hair way over to one side.

The station meant the train and the train meant New York. A year earlier my mother had taken me there to see the Christmas windows and lights. Hold my hand, she'd warned, I don't want you getting lost. We were in a human surge—shoppers, beggars, hotdog and pretzel vendors, bell-ringing Santas—everyone tall and loud and fast, bumping against each other so that suddenly I wasn't holding anyone's hand and the woman beside me was a stranger.

I didn't know what to do. I stood in the nearest doorway, a tobacco store, and waited. How long would it take for her to notice? And what if she didn't come back? I'd read some Dickens, knew about orphans, workhouses, buckets of slop, the way adults could just disappear. My father for one.

People streamed by. I looked for her coat, its fake fur collar, her white vinyl boots and red hair. Santa rang his bell, the shop door opened, shut, people went where they went, I stayed where I was, then she was yanking my arm, yelling I told you, I told you to hold on, her long hair falling into my face, sticking to my cheeks. And now any minute she'd shout Surprise! We're all going to Steak 'n Brew, just let me change into something decent.

Lucky jingled his keys.

Eleven o'clock, my mother told Roy. She kissed us both. You two have fun.

I got in the back of Lucky's VW. It smelled of liverwurst and beer. The floor was sticky.

Why can't we take your Cadillac? I asked and Roy said it was because there was nowhere to park. It had begun to drizzle, something between ice and rain, not one thing or the other. From inside his jacket Lucky took out a flask and downed a swig.

Better hurry, Roy said.

Lucky, all obliging, peeled out of the driveway, ran two stop signs, swerved around a pedestrian, went into a skid, and nearly rammed into a tree.

Man, that was close! He took another drink.

Let me hold that. Roy put the flask in the glove compartment.

In school they'd shown us movies where crash test dummies go hurtling through windshields, every make believe bone in their crash test dummy bodies shattered. I'd put on my seatbelt and had bent forward the way the movies showed you were supposed to. Whether or not I believed in God was a thing I hadn't figured out yet but in my head I was saying something like Please God oh please don't let us crash.

The train was leaving the station.

Damnit! Roy said. Wait here. He slammed the passenger door.

Lucky turned on the radio. He took the flask from the glove compartment, but it was empty. A train pulled into the station. People stepped off, opened umbrellas; women in rain scarves stood by their cars and waved. A man with a briefcase, home early for better or worse, stayed on the platform, scanning the parking lot. Poor bastard, Lucky said, meaning the man or himself or the world in general. He started singing along to Otis Redding, whistling at the whistle parts, wasting time.

The next train wasn't for fifty minutes. Roy knew a place we could wait.

Okay, Lucky said, gotta go, have a great time, see you later, have
fun, talk to you tomorrow, so long, his words pushing us into the
drizzly night where it would just be me and Roy, alone on our date,
whoever's bad idea it was, whatever reason lay behind it, when Roy,
maybe beginning to have doubts of his own, said, What's your hurry?
I'm buying.

They got whiskeys. Roy ordered me a rum and Coke without the
rum and gave me a handful of nickels for the jukebox. I flipped
through titles, staring into the jukebox's cold white light, imagining
myself the singer of these songs I knew so well, songs about new love,
broken love, false love, baby love, trying to make myself if not exactly
invisible then into someone else, someone who was not afraid of
monkeys and strangers and bad smelling men with flasks. Four nickels, five songs, and we were on the train, all those Connecticut towns
slipping past, Roy ignoring my questions, where mostly, but also
what and when, as towns yielded to city, houses to apartments, fire
escapes hard by the tracks, houseplants in a window, a flash of someone's face, until we were in the tunnels below Grand Central, walking
into the station with its Zodiac-painted dome, a huge illuminated
Kodak ad showing a happy family in the snow, while in the waiting
hall men snored on benches. Roy took my hand. His hand was warm,
warmer than my mother's, whose hand was always so cool and
lotioned and smooth. The band of his high school ring pressed into
my palm.

Rain streaked the taxi's windshield, blurring the traffic lights. My
wool coat felt damp and safe. Roy was saying how there wasn't time
to eat, maybe later we'd grab some pretzels. We turned a corner and
that's when I saw the sign, the column of red neon that spelled
RADIO CITY.

For years I'd been pestering my mother to take me to Radio City
Music Hall, ever since seeing The Rockettes on the Macy's Parade.
Alone in my room I practiced high kicks, arms outstretched, touch-
ing the powdered shoulders of my imaginary chorus line partners. In

my excitement, I forgot that Roy's crimes outweighed his good points four to one, that he hung around our house all day abandoning poor Ranger and making rules.

I followed him into the lobby. Red velvet walls, lipstick-shaped chandeliers, curvy balconies, all this was new to me. The ninety-nine cent theater at home had torn seats, stale popcorn, graffiti scratched into bathroom stalls. Look, Roy said, pointing to the carpet, the guitars and saxophones and banjoes woven there. We walked up the grand staircase towards a mural where a Biblical looking man leaned on a staff at the foot of a mountain. Far above gods zoomed past in chariots, too busy or important to notice this speck of a man stuck on Earth. We climbed past him, one more flight. A movie had just ended; the credits were rolling. But I didn't care about any movie.

We found our seats. The lights rose and dimmed. I grabbed Roy's arm as The Rockettes filed onstage. They were ladies in hoop skirts, gliding through some snowy Ye Olde village. They were Santas, reindeer, elves. Finally they lined up and became The Rockettes, high kicking toy soldiers, tiny as the man in the mural, toppling backwards, one by one.

I clapped until my hands stung. Animals lumbered onstage— camels, sheep, the manger's menagerie. The good part was over. The movie screen came back down. A cartoon cat and her kittens wandered homeless around Paris, under the protection of a scruffy tomcat. Every once in a while one of them sang about their predicament.

Roy leaned towards me, so close I could smell his Old Spice, his whiskey and Juicy Fruit breath.

You like this? he asked.

Not really.

Good, let's go.

That movie, he said, when we were back on the street, was nothing that can't be rectified by a good meal. So I didn't understand what we were doing in an office building elevator, headed to the sixty-fifth floor.

I knew about restaurants, of course. That they were bright noisy places with waitresses in aprons, color photos on the menu to help you decide, maybe even a salad bar. I knew about church, too, the votives and printed programs, hushed voices, special clothes. They were separate worlds, distinct, yet here they felt confused. We were led through a vast room to a table by a floor-to-ceiling window. The rain had stopped, fog settling in. Building lights appeared and vanished—Chrysler, Empire State, those urban constellations.

I searched the menu for familiar words. Because it sounded pretty, I chose rainbow trout. Roy ordered a Manhattan and steak, medium rare. He lit a cigarette. I made a show of waving away the smoke but everyone else was smoking too, and the smoke and candle flames and fog, the shining plates and knives, had a hypnotic effect, as though I were trapped some place between sleeping and waking.

All around us couples ate noiselessly, not seeming to move their lips: pearly women, smooth-faced men with cufflinks and clunky watches. Roy didn't wear a watch because time, he claimed, was a force of oppression, a philosophy not shared by my mother, who was always saying things like Hurry up and It's time someone went to bed.

My fish turned out to be just that: a fish in its entirety, looking nothing like a rainbow. A cloudy yellow eye stared at me; I covered it with lettuce. What were we doing here, me in my cowboy boots and corduroys, Roy talking as he chewed, an accident scene in his mouth?

A woman my mother's age, beautiful like her, lifted her glass. Light glinted off her bracelets. Perhaps some future me was already here, waiting, a woman with upswept hair, a low cut dress, a woman lifting her glass in a toast. As her, I'd know every word on the menu and—this was important—what to expect. The man with me would take me to an apartment with a view just like this, because all of the views would be just like this. I sipped my Shirley Temple, pretending it was champagne, which was easy since I'd never tasted champagne.

Having fun? Roy asked.

Sure, I said. And it wasn't a lie, not really. I knew there had to be a reason why he was showing me this world of chandeliers and showgirls. So I wasn't entirely surprised when Roy said That's good because your mother and me we both thought it was time we got to know each other, now I'm going to be your Daddy.

That was not the surprise. The surprise was why my mother had not chosen to tell me this herself. Why it was Roy and not my mother sitting across from me, saying words to change my life. What was she doing now? Soaking in the bath? Reading magazines, drinking wine? Was she sitting at her vanity, brushing her long red hair, glad to have me out of it, if only for a night?

Well? Roy said.

What's going to happen to Ranger?

That's all you have to say?

It seemed important though. What with all the dogs and cats and goldfish in the world I knew that Ranger didn't stand a chance. Who would want him?

He'll go live at the zoo.

What zoo?

A figure of speech, darlin'. A hypothetical if you will.

I hated when Roy talked that way, showing off. I made a note to add it to my list.

We don't have a zoo, I said.

We had desserts, after dinner drinks—cognac, hot chocolate. We'll call your mother from the station, Roy said, and we would have except the train was just leaving and how were we to know it was an express? Did the announcement board say so? Did the conductor? This is what he asked my mother when she came to get us in New Haven, four towns away and two hours past curfew. She said nothing in response.

Only when I was in bed did I hear her screaming, words I'd over-heard years before, huddled beneath the covers late at night: respon-sibility and fuck up and trust. I knew even then that she was right. She was right about Ranger, too, and about Roy. But I couldn't help wishing that she was wrong.

I got my diary from my dresser. In blue I wrote:

3. Took me to see the Rockettes.

Then in red:

9. Always showing off with big words—it sounds stupid.

Long ago, when he was in a good mood, my father used to toss me in the air. Beanbag he called it. Come here my little Beanbag, and he'd hoist me high above his head while I kicked and shrieked in mock fear. Don't let go, I'd cry, and he'd laugh and say Never. I still remember that feeling, the ground giving way, the rush of air, the safety of being held, still have dreams even now where I am falling only there's no one to catch me and I wake up just in time.

My mother kept screaming. I put the diary away.

In the morning Roy would be gone, back to his other life, the one with Ranger and the futon couch. Or he'd be at the kitchen table, stirring sugar into his coffee, cracking jokes, trying to coax a smile from my mother. There was no way to know. His showing off didn't seem so important after all, but I'd written the words in ink and they could not be erased.

Tomorrow, I thought. Tomorrow I would come up with something to write in blue, something to shift the balance just a little bit. There would be plenty of time.

Griswold

People confused them, one for the other. Those matching play-suits in scratchy seersucker, those fringed blonde bangs. Which one are you? a neighbor might ask, and if the younger sister spoke her name, the neighbor might smile and say of course.

The grandmother spoiled them, or so the mother claimed. Look what I brought you, she'd say, unzipping her vast purse, extracting workplace contraband: Day-Glo scrunchies, rhinestone encrusted barrettes, nail polish in shimmer or matte.

The girls smeared on polish, clumping it, waving their hands above their heads and shaking their hips, harem dancers.

You see, said the mother.

Nonsense! the grandmother replied.

Trouble, said the mother's new boyfriend. They'll be a handful, you bet.

The boyfriend had moved in three months earlier with a duffel bag and a box of rusty tools. He tended bar—that's where the mother had met him at an after work party with some friends. Because he worked nights they had to be quiet all day. Otherwise he'd yell from bed. For the mother he had pet names—Fish Face, Bubble Butt—but he rarely called the girls anything.

* * *

The grandmother had a present, one in its own special case.

Voila! she said, unlatching the black vinyl cylinder, lifting its lid. Inside was a mannequin head.

It's ugly! the younger sister said. Close it.

The older sister agreed, but knew better than to say. The mannequin's eyes were amber slits, the cheeks glazed with fine cracks. Its hair, pigeon colored, balding in spots, had the spun sugar look of a troll doll.

They'd seen other mannequin heads in the glass-fronted case at their grandmother's shop. Blondes, brunettes, with arched brows and kiss me lips. But this head, she knew, belonged to a witch, a witch who was angry because she wanted her body back, wanted to fly around at night making cauldrons of witches' brew.

We have to learn to work on all kinds, the grandmother said. Not all our clients can be princesses like you two.

They named the head Griswold and kept it on a high shelf at the back of their bedroom closet. At night sometimes, when the lights were out, the older sister would tease the younger one.

Hear that? she'd say, scratching at her headboard. It's Griswold trying to escape.

Quit it.

Griswold, Griswold, witch of the dark. Come forth from your hiding place.

I'm not listening, the younger sister would say and she'd turn her face to the wall.

Eat them! The older girl scraped peas onto her sister's plate. Eat them or You-Know-Who will know.

You can't scare me.

She rises from the closet at night. She feasts on children's bones. Lost to some private vision, the girl shut her eyes as she rocked back and forth.

Mom, make her stop!

The mother was washing dishes. She put down a plate and wiped her hands on her jeans.

I'm warning you two...

Not me, her. She's trying to scare me with Griswold.

Who's Griswold?

Who stole my body? the sister chanted. Who dared to do such a thing?

What the hell are you talking about? the mother said. One God damned minute of peace...

Fish Face, stop that racket!

All day the boyfriend had been sleeping. A double shift at the bar, who wouldn't be tired? the mother had said.

I mean it, he yelled. Don't make me get up.

That's it! cried the mother. I don't want to hear one more peep about Grisworth or anything else.

Griswold, the older girl said. And that's when she got her idea.

They would scare him off. Cast a spell, make him want to leave.

It'll take time, the older sister said. We'll have to turn ourselves into witches.

That's impossible, the younger one said.

But what better idea did she have?

Crouched beneath the window of the room where he slept, their knees in the dirt, they wore new wigs from their grandmother: red for the younger sister, black for the older one. Both wigs were synthetic, extravagantly fake, the red one shoulder length and curly, the black one longer, severely parted. It curtained the older sister's face, narrowing it, making her nose and chin appear sharp.

Griswold's head lay in the grass. With press-on nails the sisters clawed at the window screen. The boyfriend's snores abated then resumed in violent, choking spurts. The older sister hoisted Griswold's head level with the window.

Go from here, she intoned. Go on your cursed way.

Your cursed way, the younger one repeated. Be gone forever.

We have to wear them all the time, she explained. Otherwise the spell won't work.

But the younger sister balked.

They're hot. They're itchy. We'll get in trouble.

You want him gone, don't you?

This is stupid. You don't even know. She pulled off her wig, tossed it onto her bed. Her hair, tightly braided, was coiled into a crown and she touched it lightly as if making certain it was still there.

Now you've done it, her sister said.

She came into the kitchen, wig askew because she'd been sleeping in it. With the mother's pilfered eyebrow pencil she'd blackened her pale eyebrows and had drawn a mole on her left cheek. The mother had left for work; the boyfriend was still asleep.

You can't wear that, her sister said. She was eating the last Pop-Tart in the box and she broke off a piece for her sister.

I can if I want. She shoved the Pop-Tart into her mouth. I'm not afraid. Not like some people.

The younger girl hung back on their way to the bus, letting her sister board first, choosing a seat several aisles away. The teasing began at once. People lobbed spit balls, wadded up paper, shot rubber bands. Someone tried to stick gum in the wig but the girl, too fast, turned around and threatened to gouge her tormentor's eyes. The bus driver ignored them, immune to the everyday chaos.

On the playground the children trapped the girl in a circle. Freak! they shouted. Loser! Gulls shrieked and wheeled, dive-bombing the adjacent dump. The girl, a crazy-wigged maypole, used her elbows to ward off her attackers, her sister tugging at their shirttails, crying Stop!

What's all this? The children scattered at the teacher's voice. Take off that ridiculous thing!

The girl, refusing, was sent to the office. Her mother was called.

Half a shift down the drain, she said, dragging her daughter to the car. You think I can afford this? Think money grows on trees?

When it happened again the mother threw the wig into the trash. Your own hair will be next, she said. Plus, you're grounded.

Grounded? The boyfriend scoffed. What good will that do? Where would she even go? He unbuckled his trousers. A swift whack or two across the rear, that's what she needs.

Not now, said the mother. But someone had best mind her ps and qs.

You're too soft on her, the boyfriend complained.

Give her time, the grandmother counseled.

Why do you have to be such a weirdo? her sister asked.

The mother gained weight. At night she soaked her feet in salts; mornings she stayed in the bathroom, puking.

She's having a baby. Saying this aloud, telling her sister, the girl realized it was true.

Good, said her sister. I'll finally have someone to boss around.

Good? She couldn't believe it. Everyone knew what happened to stepchildren. They were starved, beaten, forced to live outside. They wore rags, ate gruel, probably had fleas. Nobody human loved them.

They'll put it in our room. They'll make us sleep in the cellar.

No they won't. You're making things up again.

The boyfriend would become the husband. A date was set; the sisters would be flower girls. They had new dresses—pink with lace collars. The younger one pirouetted, belling her skirt. The older one came up with a plan.

The night of the next full moon she snuck out the kitchen door. She had a flashlight, rubber gloves, paper towels, scissors. The poison ivy grew in clumps along the backyard fence. She beamed a light into the patch, snipped a few leaves at their base and sealed them in a zip lock bag. With the paper towels she tugged at the fingers of her gloves, which she hid in the trash.

The next day she wore cotton gloves. She was careful not to touch the leaves to her mother's side of the bed. Among the fairy tales she'd read was the story of the robber bridegroom—his betrothed warned to flee by the groom's caged bird—and while she worked she made up a little chant:

Turn back, turn back, thy lazy groom
Or else prepare to meet thy doom.

His eyes swelled shut. His face blistered. He had to wear dark glasses, even indoors, and could not go to work. The doctor prescribed cortisone. The mother, miraculously, escaped with a few small splotches. Of course the wedding was postponed.

Both sisters were blamed.

She tells you everything, the boyfriend said. No way you didn't know.

But I didn't, the younger one protested, and the older one swore that was true.

One after the other he stood them in a corner. The younger one went first. He ordered her to drop her pants then her underpants. She began to cry. Go easy, the mother said. When it was the older girl's turn he did not restrain himself, drawing blood. The girl bit her lip. She stared at her mother, who finally said Enough.

Her or me. They could hear him, one floor below, his voice rising through the radiator vents. The poison ivy had pitted his cheeks; the skin on his arms was darkened and rough. One or the other, he yelled. Not both.

The girls huddled together on the older sister's bed. Their mother said something soothing, her voice water cascading over rocks. The boyfriend quieted. Soon the mother began to moan, softly at first, then in high-pitched rhythmic bursts. The girls put their hands over their ears.

The mother was taking them to the beach. The younger sister had made up a song: We're going to the beach, yes we are yes we are. We're going to the beach in Mom's new car.

The car was old. Its brakes screeched. The passenger door was broken.

The older sister's suitcase was packed. The next day the mother would drive her to the other end of the state, to the school for troubled youth, the one the boyfriend called boot camp.

Camp! The younger sister wanted to come along, but the mother said no. You'll stay with your grandmother until I'm back, she said.

At the beach the mother spread striped towels, spiked an umbrella into the sand. She wore elastic-waist shorts, one of the boyfriend's t-shirts. The girls had one-piece bathing suits, red with white stars. A long welt was still visible on the back of the older girl's thigh. The mother smoothed lotion onto the girls. She lit a cigarette and sat in the shade of the umbrella, staring at the sea. Stay close to the shore, she said, but the tide was low and the girls waded, ankle deep, to a distant sand bar.

They had candy necklaces, tin pails, plastic shovels. They sucked at the beads, gritty with sand, and the younger one made a cat's cradle from the string. She tried to pass it to her sister, but her sister picked up her shovel and began to dig for beach glass. After a while the younger girl began digging too. For a long time neither of them spoke. A strand of kelp washed up, tangling itself around the older girl's thigh. She flicked it back into the sea.

Gross! her sister said. She'd found a whorled snail shell and she blew into it then held it to her ear.

Listen! You can hear the ocean.

The older girl kept digging.

I'll come visit, her sister said. Mom told me I could.

She did not respond.

She said you'll be home at Christmas and maybe won't have to go back.

The younger girl rinsed her shell in the tidal pool. She'd unearthed a few small treasures—two pieces of brown glass, a scallop shell, a sand dollar, nearly intact—and she put the snail shell in her pail with these other things.

We'll have a new sister by then, she said.

I don't want a new sister.

The older girl took the shell from her sister's pail. The sea sounded loud, like blood coursing through her ears when she ran too fast. It came from a place too far away to name. She put the shell back.

I'm not coming home. Not if he's there.

You have to. You can't stay away forever.

Who says?

She hadn't found much, just a rusted quarter and a handful of splintered clamshells that she'd tossed aside. The sun was hot on her shoulders and back and she knew that if they did not go in soon, both she and her sister would burn. Her mother would blame her for that.

You could come with me, she said. If you were bad, I mean. Then they'd send you.

Her sister seemed to consider this. She chewed on her empty necklace string.

I don't want to leave, she said at last.

The older girl was writing her name in the sand. The waves, still gentle, had begun coming in fast. They lapped at the letters, water filling the trenches the girl had dug.

You wait, she said. Just wait till they're married and that baby's born. You think he's mean now, you wait and see. They'll send you away no matter what.

Not if I'm good. Anyway, he's not all that mean. Not really. She shielded her eyes as if saluting someone and looked out to where the buoys floated in deep water. Mom likes him, she said.

Without a word the older girl stood up. She grabbed her sister's pail by the handle. She walked to the edge of the sand bar and dumped her sister's treasures into the sea. Her sister ran after her but the girl kept walking into the water. Neither girl could swim well. The waves, gray and foamy, slapped at her waist. At the horizon she could just make out the speck of a sailboat. Beyond it was more land, Europe she thought. There it was already nighttime, or maybe still morning. Families were sitting down to eat. Their food was different, their language and clothes. She imagined living there, this place in Europe, this place with castles and cows. She and her sister sat side by side on a bench at a long wooden table, strange foods on their plates, strange words in their mouths. Maybe other things would be different too.

Her thoughts were broken by her sister's screams. Without thinking she began to run, kicking up water. Her sister was pointing down at a pit where two sea slugs writhed. The slugs were pale, nearly translucent, about the size of a man's thumb. A third slug was pushing its way up from below. It wriggled, blind and slimy, in the damp sand.

Cover them up! her sister cried. Cover them up!

She scooped sand into the pail, poured it over the hole. She did this three times then stamped on the mound. The slugs were disgusting. Beneath the ground she stood on was another world, teeming with unknowable things, things that made her shiver in the heat.

They're gone, she said. It's okay.

Her sister threw a handful of rocks on the mound. I'm tired, she said. Let's go.

Net yet. Wait a little.

But her sister was already heading back to the shore, back to the place where their mother was waving them in.

To The Stranger Who Brings Flowers

Your veins aren't cooperating. With a slight tug the nurse extracted
the needle. Swelling already, bruises too, Olive could tell. Bruises on
top of bruises.

You need to drink more water. I've told you that. The nurse tied a
rubber tourniquet just above Olive's elbow. If this doesn't work, we'll
have to insert a port. You don't want that, do you?

A rhetorical question, Olive did not bother to respond.

She felt the needle going in.

Got it, the nurse said. Lucky for you.

She rehung the glucose bag on Olive's IV stand then hung the bag
with the Benadryl solution beside it. She attached the tubing that
trailed from that bag into the main IV line, set the timer, and walked
away without saying another word.

The procedure would take hours. How many, precisely, depended
on a lot of things. Whether Olive ran a temperature, for instance,
and if so, how high. Whether she became nauseous enough to vomit.
Or if the hives started up again and they needed to slow the drip. The
Benadryl was to help with that and to make Olive sleep.

Only how could she?

To her left and right machines were beeping to indicate that another
round of drugs was complete.

Nurse! someone shouted. Nurse, for fuck's sake!

The patient on her right had fallen asleep. The patient on her left
was watching a Spanish language soap opera. Two women, tiny and

polished in red cocktail dresses, shrieked at each other on the over-head set. One of them threw a fork.

Olive reclined as far as her chair permitted, until she was nearly supine. She pulled the flimsy hospital blanket up to her chin. Even with stockings, her legs felt cold. The other patients wore hoodies, jeans, battered sneakers, as if they'd given up, but Olive took care with her appearance. Low-heeled shoes, sensible of course, dresses in muted colors. This was no social event. Around her head she'd wound a scarf, turban style, heavy beige silk patterned with black elm leaves.

Today Olive faced the window and could see into the office tower across the street. Far beyond it, barely visible, a thin strip of river sparkled in the late morning sun.

Coming Loov, the other nurse chirped. That nurse was Irish, cherubic. The benign nurse, Olive had nicknamed her. She wore purple Crocs and called her patients Loov. As in, All right, my Loov, let's get you set up then. Twice Olive had been assigned to her. Mostly, though, she drew the malignant nurse. The malignant nurse took offense at Olive's balky veins. She let the machines beep longer than the benign nurse did. The malignant nurse never spoke her patients' names. She was small and brisk, her dark hair clipped short and ironed to a high sheen. Something rodent-like about her, if Olive were inclined to be uncharitable. Never had Olive seen her smile. She was afraid of this nurse.

Because today was music therapy day, a hefty blonde troubadour wandered the suite, playing requests on guitar. She wore a long turquoise skirt with tiny mirrors sewn into it, and her hair, which needed washing, nearly reached her waist. Olive recognized most of the songs, making them difficult to ignore. Someone had requested "Pretty Woman" and was singing off-key in a warbling soprano. If she could get the benign nurse's attention, ask her to turn the TV down. Or draw the curtains around her recliner. It wasn't so much to ask.

Olive shut her eyes. The Benadryl had begun to take effect, making her feel distant and warm. Guitar and television and machines blurred to a single sound, the gentle rumble of a voice, a man's voice saying her name. *Livvy, my Livvy, what kept you so long?* She was entering the kitchen through the garage door, cold air coming off her wool coat, kerchief knotted beneath her chin to protect her hair from the wind, the impending storm. She'd bought fresh donuts, the Sunday paper, last one in the store. Surprised that he was up, not yet eleven, and a pot of coffee brewing on the stove. Because lately he'd taken to sleeping in, skipping first the eight o'clock mass then the ten- thirty one, still asleep when she got home. He must be feeling better; she said so. In response he merely shrugged. *What kept you?* The way he tried to make his voice stern, it was all she could do to keep from laughing. Because she knew he was glad to see her, knew the delight they took in each other.

He filled her mug with coffee, his sleeve dangerously close to the burner, his robe too loose, what with the weight he'd lost. She'd have to buy him a new one, get him to shave, too, now his hair was growing in, stubbling his head and cheeks blue-black. Yet beneath the haggard face she could see the man he'd been when they'd met, the handsome man she leaned in to kiss, her lips touching air, his form wavering, becoming ribbony, so that she grabbed his sleeve and cried NO! No, wait! She was tugging at him even as he dissolved. She tried to stay him but her hand, encumbered by the needle, wouldn't budge. Stop fidgeting, someone chided. Someone, not him. Olive blinked. She was lying on a recliner in a too bright room, her arm connected to a jellyfish that swayed from a silver pole. A woman, familiar looking, was attaching another tube to her arm, hanging a new jellyfish from the pole. This would be the first drug, the one that made her nauseous.

Water? Fruit? The refreshment cart volunteer was making her rounds. She had mottled bananas, waxy looking apples, roast beef on thin triangles of bread. She had bottles of water, cups of apple juice. Snack? she asked. Something to eat? Olive knew she should take something, try to drink a little water, but it had been so long since she'd felt thirsty.

* * *

The old man in the corner, she'd seen him before. A relapse. Those cases were the worst, hope scraped clean. With those patients she took her time. Young ones, too. Often they got better, but it was harder to watch. The suite was off limits to children. Still, the young made their way here, the college-aged, barely past puberty, some stunned-looking parent forcing cheer: *Look they have dogs! Music! Sandwiches, honey! You want a sandwich?* It was for them that she felt the most.

Mid-shift, her feet had begun to swell. Not for her these sneakers and clogs. Nail polish, lip gloss! Were they waitresses? The starch in her collar scratched her throat. Her colleagues, she suspected, did not bother with starch.

She'd ordered a transfusion for the relapsed man, codeine for someone else. She'd made certain all of her patients had blankets, cups of water. The dehydrated woman would not drink, even after the trouble with her veins. Why people had to make things difficult for themselves she could not understand. Didn't the world provide difficulty enough?

Nurse! Olive cried, and it was the benign one who came running. Olive heaved into the metal pan. Her skin was clammy, her throat raw.

That's all right, Loov, the nurse said. You just rest. I'll leave the pan here in case.

She was so kind, that one, and Olive wished she could stay, wished to hear the gentle lilt of her voice as they spoke of trivial things—the movies, the weather, anything, really, so long as it was meaningless. A human voice in this room of machines. She had a husband, Olive knew, two teenaged boys. She'd told Olive that. About the other nurse Olive knew nothing at all.

Her insides seized again and she brought up a trickle of bile. Once before she'd been sick like this, years ago. An Atlantic crossing, an anniversary surprise. The first two nights had been rough and Olive had spent them crouched over the toilet in the cabin's tiny bathroom as wave after wave pushed against the ship with muscular force, propelling it backwards so that it seemed as if they'd never reach the far shore. And then, on the third day, the sun came out and Olive joined the other passengers on deck to breathe the clean sea air, the boat swaying so gently that it was as if the storm had never occurred.

Egg salad, black coffee. Half an hour. She could take longer, sure, she was entitled and didn't the rest of them just? But half an hour and look. Her transfusion case in a state because where was his daughter? And the dehydrated woman had developed a fever, hives rising inside her arm. She'd have to slow the drip.

You're not taking it well today, she said. I'm slowing things down a bit. You'll be here longer, but it'll go easier for you.

A new patient had come in, a girl practically. An older woman sat beside her, the mother no doubt. She and the music therapist were singing bright songs to the girl, who looked at them dully.

Please, her patient said. Please do you think you could ask them to be just a little bit quieter?

The therapist sang loudly, true enough, the mother's voice more subdued. An overweight woman in a fleecy sweater, dark moons beneath her eyes. She held her daughter's hand; what else could she do? The words they sang might be false, but false cheer was something anyway.

Maybe it's helping them. She said this out loud, the words she was thinking. Maybe it makes things a little easier. Some people, they like music.

Easier. The drip, the music. Easy, easier, easiest. What did she know, this nurse? The needle was not in her vein.

Four more months, twelve more treatments, forty-eight more bags and who knew how many sleepless nights. In the building across the street two people stood at a window. A man and a woman. The woman showed the man something on her phone and they both laughed. He touched her shoulder. She took a swig of water. Olive could be either one of them but no, she was herself, attached to these tubes, these bags, this body.

She too had once had a job, and not, she thought, so very long ago. Assessing risk, warding it off with spreadsheets and charts, puzzles she delighted to solve. Her office faced west, with sunset views in winter. A husband, such luck. Their farmhouse with its sloping plank floors and drafty windows, the scratching of unseen mice in walls. No way to get rid of them.

In her garden she'd grown the food they ate, transforming root vegetables and rough greens into braises, pies, casseroles. Her husband would set the table, decant the wine, light the tapers. Some nights, the best ones, they'd sit for hours, talking their way through a bottle while the candles sputtered and waned. Her meals so much better, he said, than anything he photographed for the upscale dining magazine where he worked. Doctored dishes, he'd told her the tricks. The way stylists substituted glue for milk in the cereal shoots. Added corn syrup to chocolate sauce to make it glossy. Salt crystals on ice cream, Vitamin C powder to make the guacamole greener. He thought it a shame to treat food that way, the deception involved, but to Olive that was not the point. Instead it was the waste that upset her—perfectly good food made foul.

Together they'd converted a spare bathroom into his darkroom, painting the walls black, installing an oversized sink and ceiling fan. Under deadline, he'd sometimes spend all night there. In the morning she'd find him asleep on the couch, contact sheets piled on the floor. Once he'd been at the kitchen table, staring through a loop at a photograph of a winter salad. Who ate salad in winter? Color photos were spread all over the table. To Olive they looked identical. She bent to kiss her husband's head and smelled the solvents on his skin.

Look, he'd said, pointing at some imperfection too miniscule for her to see. That blemish on the escarole, the edge of the frame.

Why not crop it? she'd asked. It seemed such an obvious solution. He put down the loop and looked at her, incredulous. You can't just cut out the bad parts.

Why not, she'd wondered, but she kept the question to herself.

She was administering a flush to her relapsed patient, the old man whose daughter was missing. Called me an hour ago, he was saying, his words knocking into each other, a meeting or some such knows I been waiting here all morning and now what'm I s'posed to do? How much like a baby buzzard he looked, downy-skulled and beaky, his Adam's apple a riot of agitation.

I'm sure she'll be here soon.

That's the trouble with kids. Spend all your time and money raising 'em then look! Nowhere to be found. With his untaped hand he reached for his phone, overturning the plastic cup of water on his tray table.

Goddammit! he cried. This is all just too God damned much.

Shards of glass in his voice. How did his daughter stand it? She drew the curtain between his recliner and the adjacent one, where the troublesome woman napped. Then, in violation of hospital protocol, she handed him his phone.

He fumbled with the numbers.

You do it, he said. Please?

She pressed the numbers he dictated and left the curtain closed behind her.

Where are you? he wailed. I'm sick and tired of waiting.

Olive took a taxi home, rode the elevator, that blessing, to her apartment on the seventh floor. She needed to lie down. But she was too tired to nap, too tired to return messages when she got up—friends calling on their way to yoga or a soccer game, friends headed home from work, they could stop at the supermarket, the pharmacy, did she need anything?

The day before, a neighbor had brought chicken casserole. Olive ate two bites then put the rest in the freezer. She made chamomile tea and flipped through television channels, settling on a musical, Fred and Ginger, so liquid in their finery. The plot was too silly to follow. She stretched out on the couch. When she awoke the sky was streaked red and her neck was stiff but she was relieved that she'd made it all the way through the night.

At the pharmacy the cashier stuck her thumb and index finger in her mouth, extracting a gray wad of gum. She tossed it into the wastebasket then counted out Olive's change.

Olive looked at the crumpled bills in the woman's hand. She pictured germs, tiny, amoeba-shaped things in top hat and tails: pneumonia, shingles, bronchitis, tap dancing their way from the contaminated bills onto her skin.

Use your other hand, she said.

What? The woman clicked her tongue. Gold hoops with the name Roberta scripted inside them dangled from her ears.

Your hand was in your mouth. Use your other hand.

You got a problem? the woman said.

Behind her Olive could hear the scraping and throat clearing of other customers, eager for their turn.

My mouth's as clean as yours.

Exactly, Olive said.

The woman thrust the bills at her. Here!

Please get the manager.

The cashier shook her head. Her earrings slapped her thick neck. With exaggerated slowness she put the bills down and did as Olive asked.

Fuckin' freak, she muttered.

* * *

She undressed, keeping on her locket, which she never removed, not even to shower. The water, nearly scalding, felt good. She pumiced her feet, her elbows, washed her hair, put on her robe and went into the spare room where she lay down on the single bed. Its mattress sagged in the middle. Tacked to the walls were varsity pennants and posters of race cars, one spewing exhaust, another covered in flame decals. The crazy quilt she'd stitched together over many years from patches of outgrown jeans and cotton shirts. The furniture needed dusting.

When the old man's daughter finally showed up—breathless, unkempt, apologizing about a PTA conference that had gone overlong—his frustration vanished. He took her arm, let her help him up, succumbed to her care.

She turned her face towards the wall, pulled her knees to her chest. The thing inside there, she thought of it as a pebble. A pebble had lodged in her heart; every morning she woke to it. A constant companion, it stayed with her even on the busiest days. Without it she was in danger of feeling nothing at all.

On the first day of the next round of treatment Olive did not see the malignant nurse, nor on the second or third. The first two days she was assigned to a new nurse, a grandmotherly woman who brought her extra blankets and said, unprompted, Now don't you fret. On the third day the benign nurse took over. That day was busier than usual, every recliner occupied, the nurses rushing about. Perhaps, Olive thought, her nemesis had been transferred to another department, another hospital even. Maybe she'd quit or, better yet, had been fired. Olive decided she would ask.

Before leaving home she'd guzzled nearly an entire liter of water, despite its metallic taste, a side effect she'd been warned about. Still there was trouble with her veins. Those in her left arm had collapsed, useless. The benign nurse was gentle, though, and encouraging.

You're so good at this, Olive said.

Thank you, Loov. She layered gauze over the needle and taped it to Olive's hand.

The other nurse, the one who's usually here…

Mara?

Mara. Of course, Olive thought. Mara was the woman's name. She had forgotten, a consequence, she supposed, of the various drugs. She'd been warned about that, too.

Mara, yes. You should see what she did to my arm. It was sore for a week.

The nurse said nothing.

I haven't seen her this time, Olive continued. Is she… on vacation?

The nurse frowned, as if contemplating what, precisely, to say. Probably there had been complaints. Well, Loov, she finally said, I suppose so. Yes, you could say that. Now, let's finish getting you set up.

Instantly Olive regretted the question. Suppose this nurse, her ally, was upset at her now? She might stop talking, turn solemn and cold. Olive would apologize, explain that she'd merely been curious. That she had nothing against the other nurse. She would say that. Olive's mind quieted and slowed. Fat white clouds, bruise-streaked at their edges, scudded across the sky. They moved so quickly, sped by the wind, there then gone. For a while she played the children's game of giving them shapes: a bird, a flower, a snowman, half melted.

All about her was the bustle and hum of ordinary life. A man worked on a crossword puzzle. A couple played cards. One patient had three visitors; they'd borrowed Olive's unused chair and were eating thick sandwiches from the deli.

Look! one of them squealed through a mouthful of bread. A dog! How cute!

The dog, a terrier, was clowning on hind legs. Olive had never seen this dog before. Usually there was a Labrador, a regal creature that went from patient to patient, staring ahead stoically as he allowed himself to be petted.

The terrier's trainer unleashed him and put him on the card player's lap. He licked the man's hand and the man laughed and said
Good boy! He was a thin man in jeans and a hoodie with an embossed
skull and the words Alas, Poor Yorick! printed underneath. He had a
companion, a woman, to bring him blankets and water and food, to
chat with him and play cards. What did he need with a dog?

Inside their nylon casings, Olive's legs had begun to itch. She'd
meant to wear pants, another memory lapse. To distract herself she
watched the building across the street, but today no one appeared at
the windows. She could just make out the leaden thread of river at
the vanishing point between land and sky.

One dozen eggs, an extravagance. She separated whites from yolks,
letting the latter slip down the drain, whisking the whites until they
were stiff. She dipped a battered metal measuring cup into the canis-
ter of flour, topping off the excess with a butter knife. A fine mist of
flour mounded against the side of the bowl. Gently she folded it into
the snowy peaks, careful not to over mix. Angel food, his favorite.

While it baked she soaked her feet in Epsom salt and watched the
evening news. Rain in the forecast, no matter. She dried her feet,
checked the oven. The cake had risen nicely, its burnt sugar smell
comforting in a small way. She knew the recipe by heart, had made
the cake so often that she could tell, just by looking, when it was
done. She let it cool before sliding it onto a plate to rest overnight.
Because she had the next day off she could sleep late and she did so,
rising mid-morning to a sunless sky. She remembered then what the
day was.

The cake was high and light, springy to the touch. She made a
simple glaze of confectioner's sugar and vanilla, licking the excess
from her fingers. Took her raincoat from the closet, umbrella too,
just in case. She pocketed her lighter, the pack of blue candles, leaving her hands free to carry the cake. The cemetery wasn't far. His

headstone still looked new, the marble glossy and veined. A cluster of snowdrops had sprung up at its base. Soon it would be warm enough to plant flowers. Pansies, daylilies, something she could tend to. Iris and tulip bulbs come fall.

The breeze had picked up, a hint of salt in the air. She set the plate with the cake in front of the headstone.

I've brought you something, she said. She felt awkward, a little bit shy. A woman alone with a cake. What had she been thinking? In the distance a woman was wiping a headstone with a cloth. She wore a trench coat and her head was covered with a pink floral-patterned scarf. The pack of candles, the lighter, she felt for them in her pocket. She had to kneel to arrange the candles, a circle of twenty pushed into the cake. The grass beneath her was scratchy and brown. The other woman had stopped her wiping to watch. There was a song to sing, a song that went with the cake, but she knew she could not manage it. She lit the candles. The small flames wavered, blue wax dripping onto icing. If he could see her somehow, give a sign. The sky was bone white. Just one small gesture. She made a wish, blew out the candles and drove away.

Olive had been wiping dirt from the engraved letters of her husband's name when she'd sensed some movement at the periphery of her vision. She stopped working to watch the strange ritual. A woman with a cake seemed to be talking to the sky. It took Olive a moment to recognize her. Once she did, she returned to her work, keeping her head bent, not wishing to be seen. She cleared dead leaves from the base of the stone, smoothing the dirt until she heard a car door shut and looked up to see the woman driving off. She'd left the cake behind.

On her way to the cemetery Olive had stopped at the florist for branches of forsythia. Every year she had forced them to life indoors and every year her husband made the same joke. Spring in the air!

he'd cry, then do just that, a small, exuberant leap that never failed to make her laugh. She piled the branches ankle deep on the ground. The day was bitter and her head, despite its covering, felt cold. She'd have to leave soon. Grass crackled underfoot as she made her way past rows of headstones and crossed the cemetery road to where the woman had been. The cake was on a black-rimmed ceramic plate, the kind of plate sold in boxed sets at the supermarket. A simple Bundt cake drizzled with icing, ringed with blue candles. An amateur cake, something vulnerable about the way it stood out from its surroundings. Squirrels would devour it, mice and rain taking what was left. She thought about the woman who had made it and felt a fresh surge of dislike. The birthdate on the headstone was that day's date twenty years earlier. The second date was nearly a year old. They had this in common then. Yet her husband had been in his sixties. They'd met when she was barely older than this boy whose grave she stood in front of now. All those decades together. She'd had that, at least.

The cemetery road curled around monuments and mausoleums to a flat plot of land where the smaller graves were clustered. She drove slowly, past the gatehouse, the flag-pocked veterans' slope, past the stone angel with its chipped wing and puzzled expression, veering right at the pond, and that's when she saw it, a blur of incandescent yellow. Thinking sparks, fire, she sped up, braking hard at the grave. But it was only forsythia, a pyre of branches, carelessly heaped. She picked one up, its petals waxy and damp. Overhead a crow was cawing. Early morning, no one else about.

Twice more this occurred. Then for several weeks nothing, until the lilacs. Their papery hulls still held a trace of perfume. Overpowering flowers, she'd never cared for them. He, certainly, would not. The tulips she'd planted were just shooting forth their first leaves. Orange they'd be, his favorite color, like the hot rod on the poster in his bedroom, with its flame decals.

She took the dented watering can from the trunk of her car and brought it to the spigot. Today, a Saturday, other people were tending graves. A man stood, hat in hand, his coat open to the warm afternoon. A woman, her face concealed by a floppy hat, tugged at weeds. Two children ran, shrieking, in circles. She paid them no mind. But when the lilacs appeared a second time, she felt moved to respond.

That night she sat at her desk, staring at a blank sheet of good stationery, the heavy cream paper with her initials in block print. Only what to write? She'd never been good with words. Other nurses chatted easily with their patients but somehow she could never. And who was to say they would want that, a chatty nurse, taken up as they were with the raw business of survival? Sometimes she wondered: would she, herself, fight so hard? Knowing how sick it made them, how likely they were to return? Because there was something to be said for giving in, some measure of grace.

Whoever you are, she wanted to write, I know you must feel what I feel. But how could that be true? A parent, a spouse, how could it be the same? They were likely grieving the past, while she mourned the absent future. Still, the deed was kind. I don't know why you're doing this, she wrote, or even who you are, but I thank you. He was—is— my son. I miss him every day. She did not sign her name. On the envelope she wrote To the Stranger Who Brings Flowers. She sealed the card, brought it to the gravesite, and left it behind, weighted with a rock. She hoped the woman, for she felt certain it was a woman, would find it before the next rain.

The nurse looked bad. Bone snap thin, scarecrow haired, some blueprint of a self. She was checking another patient's wrist band against the information attached to his infusion bag.

Name? she asked. Date of birth?

Beneath her blanket, Olive shivered. For days the air had been mossy and still. This morning, though, the wind had picked up.

Trash scuttled along the sidewalk; heat lightning gleamed in a gunmetal sky.

The rain, when it came, was torrential. Pneumonia weather. Perhaps this explained the vacant recliners, people calling to reschedule, afraid of catching cold. But Olive would not cancel, not so close to finishing, the first day of her final round. After this, her doctor said, they would watch and wait. Olive wondered how that differed from simply living.

The Benadryl had been ordered, her temperature and blood pressure noted, her weight loss remarked upon. If her platelet count was deemed adequate they would proceed; if not, she'd be sent home for a week. Once, early on, that had happened and Olive had felt a sense of shame spasm her gut as though she'd been caught cheating on an exam. One more week, one more day, one more morning; she didn't think she had it in her. For so long she'd anticipated this moment, the jubilation of ending, but it was the dread of beginning she now felt, the shapelessness of days to come.

The troubadour was back and singing "Pennies from Heaven." Her hair, her skin, they shone with health. Her voice was loud and bright.

God damned lies, Olive muttered.

Sorry? The nurse looked at her. Do you need something?

What? She hadn't realized she'd been thinking out loud. Embarrassed, she began to fiddle with the buttons on her remote control.

No, nothing, she said. The nurse was still staring. It's just . . . that song, those words. It's nothing, really.

The nurse scowled. A mistake giving voice to her thoughts. She should have paid attention.

Ridiculous, she said. Rain is rain. Not pennies, not rainbows, not candy. It's just what it is, that's all.

Olive nodded. She understood. Of course she understood.

* * *

The patient was waiting for her lab report. Too low a count and they'd send her home, a pity really, after all this time. The treatment had taken its toll. It was evident in the looseness of the woman's clothes, low ride of skirt on bony hips, the yellow cast to her skin, made worse by the unfortunate head scarf, maroon with dusky pink roses. The scarf reminded her of something, though she could not say what. The woman did not flaunt her baldness as some of them did. She took care with her appearance. Polished shoes, tailored clothes, headscarves in contrasting hues. Probably she'd been pretty once. She had that aloofness of the favored.

When the numbers came back from the lab she prepared the bags for glucose and Benadryl. The crooks of the woman's arms were shadowed blue, the backs of her hands desiccated. But there, on the left hand, between the woman's second and third knuckles, was a promising sliver of vein. The woman made a fist. It would work.

She slid in the needle, just below the woman's gold band. Strange she'd not noticed that before. So she was married, this woman. Or had been, more likely, since there was no evidence of a spouse. A widow then. So many of them were. The woman had averted her gaze from the needle, lowering her head slightly, as if in prayer. And then, with a sharp intake of breath, she knew. The absent spouse. The scarf. That face in profile. Those dusky roses, floating above a headstone on the other side of a cemetery road. Like frosted roses on a wedding cake; she'd thought so at the time. It was her. It had to be. Only . . . why?

She finished quickly, walked away. She felt dizzy. This woman was nothing to her. A patient. They came and went, relentless in their need, three new ones for each one who was discharged. As soon as they were released she forgot them. The unfortunate ones returned and if they asked Do you remember me? she said, Of course I do.

In the nurses' lounge she made herself a cup of tea. Someone had left an open tin of cookies on the counter by the sink. A gift from a patient, no doubt. The mug she drank from was decorated with sailboats and clouds. That, too, had been a patient's gift, presented to her filled with jellybeans, which she'd tossed away.

On the street below people entered and exited shops, hailed taxis, talked on phones, maneuvering around each other, never quite touching. Sleepwalkers, she had the urge to shake them, to shout Pay attention; nothing's as ordinary as it seems.

She blew steam from her mug. The woman—Olive, that was her name—had anyone ever escorted her home? She could not recall. The nurses' lounge was cold, the air conditioner set too high again. She'd have to get her sweater from her locker. Her patients, the older ones especially, complained about the cold, becoming upset if they ran low on blankets. Who could blame them, really? The tea helped. She took a final sip, and that's when she had her idea.

She got a paper cup from the stack by the cooler, filled it with hot water, then changed her mind. A real mug, that was better. The one she'd brought from home with the logo of the university at the other end of the state. She fixed a cup of mint tea with just a touch of honey and put two cookies on a small paper plate.

The woman was asleep, her head cocked to one side. It wouldn't do to wake her. When she opened her eyes she'd find the tea and cookies and wonder at their presence. Or perhaps not. Perhaps, like so many people, she simply took things for granted. She felt a twinge of annoyance. Never mind. She would leave her gift, this token of gratitude, let the woman think what she would. About the flowers she'd say nothing. After this week the woman would be gone. If she was lucky there would be no reason for her to return. If she was lucky, they would never see each other again. Mara hoped that this would be so.

Value Added: A More Fabulous You!

First thing was my hair was disappearing. Each morning, in the shower, handfuls came loose from my scalp. I'd pull entire Chia pets from the drain, wrap them in tissue and toss them away.

Breakage, said Jack. He swiveled his hairdresser's chair so I was in profile: a wan woman, pink-smocked, too much nose, too little chin. Jack combed out a damp section, pulled it taut.

Blondes have thin hair, he said.

I'm not blonde.

We could fix that. He snapped his fingers.

God knows what possessed me. Change the color, Jack said, that's what people will see. Platinum, don't be timid. He swiveled me to face him—his own hair dark, ample, gelled stiff. We'll reshape it, too.

Jack painted my hair with a solution that reeked of ammonia. He wrapped my head in foil and I sat like that, in the window of Hair Today, flipping through magazines, reading articles like "Value Added: Invest in a More Fabulous You!" which contained tips on where to find hand-milled French soaps at forty dollars a bar, how to apply gold-flecked eye shadow "for those 24-carat occasions" and why a simple toe-straightening procedure was a must for the new summer footwear. I read "Plastic Surgery Successes" featuring The Human Barbie Doll and a couple who, after getting plastic surgery, decided to sign up their children, too, so that they would look more like a family.

I did not want to stop reading.

Time's up, Jack said. He peeled back the foil and began to cut. My hair, when he finished, looked terrific and completely wrong. It looked as though it had sprouted cherub wings, lifted itself from Miley Cyrus's head and, fluttering briefly, plopped itself down on my skull. Miley—now that was a blonde's name! Miley, Marlena, Marilyn, Mae. Not Sarah. A woman one hundred and twenty-seven years old, practically barren and married to the biggest grouch in the Bible. Or the dessert lady, the one whose bland portrait appears on boxes of cheesecake, coffee cake, what have you. Or a woman who teaches Freshman Composition and the occasional theme course (Man and Lit, Man and Society, Man Woman Lit and Society) at a community college whose students (bleary-eyed, sulking) pretended not to notice that their professor had just gone all femme fatale.

Perhaps they simply didn't care. There was that. Perhaps like my colleagues, crammed together in the adjunct office, which was the name given a converted storage room, they mistook indifference for discretion.

Look at you! This, the biggest reaction I got, came from The Frilly Poet, a fossilized woman in ruffles and pearls who lorded it over the rest of us because in addition to comp she taught an introductory creative writing course each spring and had published a chapbook, long since consigned to that limbo where out of print books languish. The Frilly Poet's husband was an acquisitions lawyer, though she was mum about what it was he acquired. She didn't need to work—she told us this—especially as she had a lucrative sideline writing greeting card verse. Lucrative, her word. Nevertheless she'd been at the college approximately one hundred years. If she ever retired I was in line to teach her creative writing course, a thing she knew and disliked me for, I could tell, by the comments she made. Comments like, Oh, Sarah, are you teaching comp *again* this semester?

The Frilly Poet and I shared a desk with two other adjuncts, but we'd each been assigned our very own mini locker. Mine was on the top row; I had to stretch to reach the combination lock. And that was the second thing. Because, you see, I was shrinking.

How long this had been happening I could not say. One day, months ago, I nearly tripped over my jeans which, I noticed, were dragging the ground. I switched to higher heels. I rolled back my sleeves, hiked my pants and began belting them above my waist. I stood on tiptoe to reach the cupboards. When that no longer worked, I used a milk crate.

Osteoporosis, I told the doctor. I'm disappearing as we speak. Plus there's my hair.

She had my chart on a clipboard and she made a little mark with her gold-plated pen. You're thirty-seven, she said. No way you have osteoporosis.

Look at me! I uncrossed my arms, letting them drop to my sides, my hands disappearing into my sleeves. This used to fit!

You should go shopping, she said.

But she ordered some tests. X-rays, blood work. For twenty-four hours I peed into a jug. Everything came back normal.

I decided I was working too hard. All that schlepping of books and student papers on the subway was making me hunched over. A forty-minute commute, standing the entire time because who gives up a seat to a perfectly healthy looking thirty-seven year old woman whose only visible affliction is the wrong kind of hair and clothes that are noticeably too large? Like maybe I was some kind of trend-setter or, more likely, behind the urban curve, racing to catch up. People stared, quickly looked away. Kids snickered. I concentrated on the subway ads—breast augmentation, dermabrasion, Caesar's Palace Atlantic City: "Moderation Has Its Place And It's Not Here" *here* being, in fact, the Bronx-bound number two train. I thought of all the things I'd do when the semester ended. I'd fly to Paris, drink unbelievable wines, swim topless in the Mediterranean. I'd rent a house on the shore, any old shore, gorge on lobster and clams. I'd write poetry, go hiking, learn to paint.

The truth was I had no plans.

* * *

My students were revising their final papers. Topic: Someone who influenced you. Sample sentence: "He was my mentor who more or less didn't give a shit about me but I had to give a shit about him because he owned the business and everyone in it." I spent most of the weekend reading these. On Monday we had a meeting with the department chair. Throughout the year we'd been receiving increasingly dire memos from an administration worried about the possibility that the adjunct faculty might actually unionize. It had happened already at a nearby school. So far our own campus was a hotbed of passivity, but the administration was taking no chances. We'd been warned—in writing and repeatedly—about the hazards of collective bargaining. How it would erode the special nature of the student/teacher relationship, how crass commercial concerns would demean the value of our product. There was talk of streamlining, of "enhancing the commitment that exists between administration and faculty" and, should that commitment fail to materialize, of giving the latter "the freedom to forge successful careers in other venues."

The Frilly Poet was sympathetic to these missives. Union people, she sniffed, simply want to bite the hand that feeds them. I imagined her whipping out a series of anti-union greeting cards with messages like:

Sorry You Were Fired

Too bad, my dear, you were let go.
You thought that this place needs you?
But it's unwise, I guess you know,
To bite the hand that feeds you.

The department chair had called the meeting to "wrap things up" and "discuss matters of some recent concern." Each May our contracts expired and we were given a letter explaining that we would be rehired "pending review of departmental needs." So far I'd racked up four of these letters. The contract expiration, the chair assured us, was "a mere formality." Certainly there'd be some "reshuffling," perhaps even some "consolidation." But no one should worry. She asked if we had any questions. We had none. Any issues? I kept my mouth shut, having seen how people with "issues" tended not to return. I sat up straight, taking pretend notes, trying to appear eager, intelligent, tall. My hair was still falling out, leaving fuzzy patches that made me look like an Easter chick.

And you, Sarah? The chair gave me the barest of smiles. How was your semester?

Just peachy, I answered. Everything's fine.

That afternoon I stood on a chair clearing out my locker. The Frilly Poet was talking to a student, an earnest looking young woman in a t-shirt with the word "Juicy" splayed across her chest.

Point of view, The Frilly Poet was saying. It's all over the place.

You don't like the story?

No, no, the story's fine. There's a problem with point of view is all. Remember, in class, we discussed the narrative guise?

The student snapped her gum. Narrative guys? she said sweetly. I don't remember them.

Quickly I stuck my head into the cave of my locker. It was musty in there, reassuringly dark. I thought about crawling inside, maybe putting down a blanket, taking a nap. How long before I would fit?

Something had to be done. My doctor was on vacation. The world was on vacation. I stayed inside my rent stabilized sixth floor walkup watching television: *Billions. A Billion to One.* Even, in a fit of nostalgia and a nod to inflation, *How to Marry A Millionaire* on the public station. I kept the blinds shut, aimed the fan at the couch and lay there, reading detective novels, trying to revise my way through a stack of poems. In grad school I'd been selected for a moderately prestigious literary award. The judge had said my manuscript showed promise, a word that made me wince. Nevertheless I'd sent the promising poems into the world and a couple of them appeared in journals that two or three people might actually have read and, encouraged, I wrote some more poems and sent those out too, thus beginning my collection of slips with "Sorry" scrawled on them and maybe someone's initials, probably a grad student intern who'd been told her work shows promise. Lately, though, nothing had been coming back, not even a generic rejection slip. My poems simply vanished into the slush pile where I imagined them living it up, carousing at night with the other slush poems, swapping one liners and having a ball.

Some days, when I wasn't writing or watching TV, I made phone calls. Summers were the roughest time, ramen noodles and lentils time. I tried temp agencies. I called the test prep place where for the past two summers I had been tutoring until it was discovered that after working with me, my students scored an average of fifty points lower on their SAT math exams. For a while I switched to the LSATs, but the logic questions proved too much.

Sample question:

"A college education can provide the pathway to a better, more prosperous life. However, the cost of tuition can prove prohibitive. Financial aid, therefore, should be linked to programs that offer a higher return on investment as indicated by the amount of time it takes a student to recover their tuition costs.

"Which of the following indicates a flaw in this logic?"

There followed a barrage of statistics about tuition rates, public vs. private institutions, STEM vs. The Humanities, etc.

Faced with this information, I asked myself—what would a reasonable person do? A reasonable person, I reasoned, would never get herself into this situation, my situation to be precise, deep in debt, living on ramen and Popsicles, using a dictionary to sit at the table and making calls that I knew would go unreturned. Which is why I was surprised, after leaving my phone to charge while I trudged off to the market, to find myself with not one but three voicemails. Midweek, mid-afternoon, this was call back prime time. A temp agency with a job to get me through August. Or a magazine—they wanted my work, all of it, and would I send more? The chair—late July, no word yet about my contract, she was calling to apologize—how could she have overlooked me? A robot telemarketer—that seemed more likely—three of them, proffering e-z credit, cut rate cable, bulk rate electric, all you can eat, offer ends soon, don't delay. Which it was. At least the first call. The second was in Chinese. The third I recognized instantly from the Church of England by way of Little Rock accent. My sister-in-law. Would I come to their housewarming party? Cocktails, barbecue, nothing fancy. Looking forward, she chirped. Oh, and please, no gifts.

But I wasn't falling for that. No gifts—I knew the lexicon. Show up empty-handed at your peril. Only what to get a pharmaceuticals executive and his pseudo-British Bible Belt wife who, in addition to owning a country home furnished with Shaker antiques had just acquired a seventeen room brownstone? A butler? A gazebo? Would anything smaller be perfect enough? I settled on lavender—English lavender for Amanda's garden. I belted a t-shirt to make a dress, put the potted lavender in a shopping bag and rode the train out to leafy, low-slung Brooklyn. The house was on a one-way street that was a central casting version of Victorian America if Victorian America had had Mini Coopers. I climbed the stoop, stretching slightly to reach the door knocker.

Amanda met me in the foyer, glanced at my plant and said, We'll just stick that outside. A mahogany table was piled with gifts; the ones that wouldn't fit were heaped on the parquet floor. Some had already been opened. Lenox china, Baccarat crystal—wedding gifts for marriage to a house.

I'd worn my highest heels and I teetered slightly as I followed Amanda through living room, dining room, kitchen, out the back door, into the garden. White hydrangeas banked a grille-work fence. A brick walkway bisected the yard, making a trail straight to Amanda's rose garden whose bushes, I noticed, all bore white flowers. There were mosaic tables, Adirondack chairs, cigar smoking men deep in leisure, women in jewel-toned silks though Amanda wore white, emphasizing her tan. There were children and they scampered, really scampered, like baby cartoon animals. My nephews, twin blurs, came charging at me.

Auntie Sarah! they cried, tackling me so that I struggled to stay aloft on my ridiculous heels. Three-year-old Rex and Roy, I could not tell them apart.

Boys! I said. Boys whoa! Look at you. You're getting so big, tomorrow you'll be bigger than your Auntie. It wasn't a joke, only how were they to know?

We're in school! they chimed.

Did I tell you? Oh, yes. Amanda stooped to wipe mustard from a mouth, kept her knees bent, the better to address me. They passed their preschool interviews, just last week. Who are the two smartest little boys in the whole wide world?

We are! We are! They jumped, not quite in unison. Auntie Sarah, come play. Did they think I was a toy? A peer, perhaps? Still their offer was tempting. They could take turns pushing me in the hammock while I sipped mint juleps.

Auntie Sarah needs a drink, I said.

But Amanda commandeered me by the arm. Come say hello to Steve, she said.

My brother, Lord Buddha, was flipping steaks. He was bigger than ever, bigger even than when I'd last seen him, at Thanksgiving, jovially dismembering a turkey. Sarah! he cried, pulling me into a one-armed bear hug, his other arm waving the spatula, dripping grease. My head was pressed into his paunch and I wondered, not for the first time, how he came to be that way—the Buddha, I mean—a skin-and-bones mendicant transformed somehow into a beatific Eastern Santa Claus. Who made him so fat?

Steve squeezed me until I gasped. He smelled of sweat, aftershave, lighter fluid, a reassuring smell. The rayon of his Hawaiian shirt felt damp against my cheek.

You look great! he boomed. I wriggled free, gulped for air.

Steve, I said, I'm shrinking.

It's this God damned heat. I'm melting away too. He loaded the steaks onto a platter and they really did make that sizzling noise just like in commercials.

No, I mean it.

What you need is a nice cold drink. He pointed his chin towards a corner of the yard I'd already scoped out, a corner where most of the adults had chosen to congregate. Glasses and bottles and little bowls of drink accessories were displayed on what looked like a massive altar, one of Amanda's flea market finds, no doubt.

I wobbled over, goal in sight. The array of bottles was impressive and though I only wanted one, and wasn't even particular as to which one, I wanted it badly.

Scotch was in front. I chose Scotch. Jewelry flashed at eye-level—bracelets, rings, watches—icy and substantial. The scotch burned going down. I poured another. If I drank myself under the table, at least I wouldn't have far to go.

And then I really was under it, the table, or just about, sprawled on my ass, Scotch pooling around me.

Oh! Amanda squealed. I didn't see you. It was an accusation. I hoisted myself up and held on to the table, waiting for the world to steady itself. Someone had moved the Scotch, so I fixed myself a gin and tonic to help clear my head.

Sar-ah, Amanda drawled, the heat evidently loosening the syrup in her voice, c'mon with me. Her fingers on my shoulders were little pistons steering me into her coterie of women. This, she announced, is Steve's sister.

The women smiled, so many perfect teeth!

Sarah's a teacher, Amanda said blandly.

Really? What? someone asked dutifully and on cue.

English. I'm a poet.

Oh. Poetry. From her tone she may as well have said Oh. Ebola.

It's all too lit'rary for me, Amanda opined, as though she'd actually read any of my work. Anyway, we have a mission. She strode to the head of our little clique. Ready for the tour?

Back we went through kitchen-dining room-living room, up two flights of stairs to our first stop: Steve's billiard room which, Amanda mock-complained, he insists on calling pool. We saw the walk-in cedar closet, the stained glass window in the guest bathroom, the library with its floor-to-ceiling bookcases, waiting to be filled. The ceiling could be just a smidge higher, Amanda said, just a couple of inches. Meaning, I supposed, an even hundred feet.

The women ooohed and cooed. They had the same vocabulary lists: Viking, Sub-Zero, Stickley. Away they burbled, these swans in barbecue silks, making their pleasant watery sounds just above my head.

Down and down the stairs we trooped into the wine cellar. So cool in there, I wanted to stretch out on the tile floor. As if hearing my thoughts, a woman in emerald silk said, Oh, I could just move in here, set up a cot and stay through Labor Day.

Yes, it's been so beastly, a ruby silk concurred. If we weren't going away, I'd grab a corkscrew and join you.

But we'll be at the shore! Emerald protested, as if to say How *could* you think otherwise? And you, my dear, you'll be upstate, won't you? It's a shame you don't care for the ocean.

With my complexion! Amanda clapped a hand to her breast. Besides... those crowds...

Well, Ruby interrupted, wherever you go, you'll be somewhere, that's the main thing. I almost did a double take. Who'd let one of my students into the room?

August is always so miserable. This from a sapphire silk who'd managed to make the word miserable sound like a treat.

I certainly hope so. Otherwise, what's the point in getting away?

Who said this? I don't recall. To my surprise, someone answered, I know what you mean. Whenever I go out to eat, if I think about all the starving people in the world it makes the food taste so much better. To my bigger surprise, that someone was me.

The women all looked down. What was this pip-squeak doing in their midst? Amanda crinkled her nose. Well, she said, all sugar drained from her voice, we really should keep moving. Single file the women followed her out. But I stayed behind, lingering in the cool dim cave. If I was lucky—and why wouldn't I be?—no one would notice I was missing. I could stay here all summer, wine enough to last for years. Come winter I'd hibernate, curled up behind shelves, an animal shrinking in its lair, until the day someone at last discovered me, tiny as a newborn, and led me blinking and reluctant back into the cold.

All You Wish For

She was looking for clues—where he might have gone and why. Good riddance, was all her mother would say. For cryin' out loud, leave it alone; that was her sister.

Her parents' closet smelled of mothballs and musk, grassy traces of her mother's good perfume. She tugged, twice, on the slack string attached to the overhead bulb. Her mother's side of the closet was thick with housedresses in an array of noncolors: beige, ivory, rust. Starched to woodenness, they reminded her of chess pieces. Espadrilles and Capezios pointed, toes down, in a canvas shoe bag. Her father's side was empty, his shoe bag a deflated gourd.

She tried to picture someone belonging to this room, undressing here nightly, tossing dirty clothes aside, loosening tucked sheets, sneaking whispered bits of conversation the way she and her sister did. The shades were pulled against the sun, curtains closed, the white duvet smoothed creaseless. Above the bed hung the room's sole decoration, a framed print of palm trees on a frothy beach. She'd never seen a beach; as far as she knew no one in her family had.

Steadying herself against the closet's lower shelf, she climbed onto her mother's tufted vanity stool. He'd left his fedora behind, the boxed after shave and soap set she'd given him for Father's Day. Beside it were the Rapunzel wig and fairy wings of her mother's last Halloween costume. On the upper shelf she found a stack of magazines. Miss April liked scuba diving and dark chocolate; she disliked mean people. The vastness of her breasts made her head look small.

The magazines were stacked on top of the Ouija board, another thing she'd never seen before.

It's a game, stupid, her sister said. They used to bring it out at parties. It can't tell you anything.

So how come it was in their room and not the hall closet with the Monopoly and Parcheesi and Scrabble? she asked. How come if it's not special?

You're not supposed to be in there, you know. What if I told?

Let's ask it something. Where he's gone.

Who cares? It's not like he's coming back.

The instructions warned not to use the board alone but, really, what choice did she have?

She took the board from its hiding place beneath her bed to the basement workroom where her father had spent most of his time and where, she reasoned, any traces of him were apt to be strongest. The workroom door, swollen with humidity, would not shut all the way. She switched on the clock radio, hoping for a classical station, music a spirit might recognize and be drawn to, but all she could find was talk radio and oldies rock. Someone singing about rambling, singing about buses and roads. She turned it off. In the kitchen utility drawer she'd discovered a stub of votive candle and she placed that on the workbench where she sat, the board on her trembling knees. At the top of the board were drawings—leering sun, frowning crescent moon—both set in dark clouds. She wasn't certain what they meant or what, if anything, she should do about them. She rested her fingertips on the plastic planchette the way the instructions said to do.

Is anyone there? she said.

Can anyone hear me?

She waited.

If anyone's here please give me a sign.

She felt the planchette slip beneath her fingers, felt it moving, ever so slowly, towards the word Yes. Perhaps she was pushing it, just a little; it was difficult to tell.

Okay, she said. Good. So...um...can I ask you something?

The candle flame flickered. She took this as an omen, another yes.

Do you know where my father's gone? she asked, getting straight to the point. Who knew how much patience existed in the spirit world?

If you know, can you say?

The planchette did not move.

Is he dead? Is he coming back? Two questions—that was bound to be confusing.

Do you know where he is? she asked again. Can you give me a sign?

With a popping noise the basement went dark. The numbers on the clock radio vanished, the dehumidifier stopped humming. She ran from the room, upsetting board and candle, and was nearly at the stairs when the lights came back on. Her sister at the fuse box, laughing.

Every day her sister told a new story.

He had a girlfriend; they'd moved to France.

He was gay and lived in California.

He stole money from work and went to jail.

He hated us, all of us, well...you, really.

Our mother, she dumped him for another man.

Their mother with her flat shoes and face, her plain dresses and terrier hair. It seemed impossible. Still, people could be different from how they seemed. And if her mother disappeared...then what?

* * *

But she was disappearing already, volunteering for extra shifts when another nurse at the community hospital went on maternity leave. Three nights a week her mother stayed away until morning, a sheet of notebook paper outlining what was to be done: meals defrosted, dishes washed, laundry folded—the demands tempered by a line of Xs and Os at the bottom of the page. Her sister stirred packaged cheese sauce into macaroni or microwaved veggie burgers that they ate from paper plates while watching TV past midnight. Sitcoms were good, old movies better, especially ones where the heroines escape danger from gangsters or fortune hunters or spies—any kind of danger, really, so long as something happened. Afternoons, if her sister was out, she'd search her mother's jackets for coins then ride her bike to the corner store for ice cream sandwiches and barbecue chips. Or she'd lie on the couch watching cartoons as light drained from the room. Did you do your homework? her mother would ask and she always answered yes.

Her mother had no change for the meter. The trip to Rite Aid, she promised, would not take long: Just, if someone tries to ticket us, tell them I'll be right back.

In the glove compartment, behind the registration and maps, her mother sometimes kept packs of gum. Today though there was nothing but some crumpled Wrigley's wrappers. She looked up from her scrounging and that's when she saw him, on the other side of the intersection, half a block away. Unmistakable, that clean-razored hairline high on his neck, the wide swing of his arms. A woman walked beside him, a red-haired woman in a turquoise striped dress.

She ran from the car shouting Dad! Hey Dad! Cars sped through the intersection, the pedestrian light beaming Don't Walk. She watched as he and the woman got into an unfamiliar sports car. They were gone before the light changed.

* * *

I saw him. Downtown when we were at Rite Aid.

You did? Her sister was paying attention for once. What did Mom do?

Mom wasn't there.

Good thing. So... what happened?

All afternoon, while her sister was at soccer practice, she'd been waiting to tell her story. She'd seen their father! He had a girlfriend, a sports car too! But now, as she began to share her news, she could feel her excitement waning. Once told, the story would be used up. Worse yet, it would no longer belong to her alone. Its power diminished with each word she spoke.

There was a woman with him. A redhead.

What did she look like?

Tall.

What else?

She had a striped dress.

No, don't be stupid. I mean... what did she look like? Was she pretty? How old was she?

I don't know.

What do you mean you don't know? Her sister was frowning. She shouldn't have told. Besides, he hadn't turned around. If pressed, could she really say for certain it was him?

Well... they were walking ahead of me.

You mean you didn't see their faces?

Not exactly.

So how do you even know it was him?

I just do. I mean... who else could it be?

I don't know. Anybody?

She was forgetting the sound of his voice. How it rose when he teased her, saying Kiddo or Princess; Holy smoke! Low with threat those times she'd neglected something—homework, a chore. The sad songs he sang late at night when she was supposed to be sleeping. Bye Bye Blackbird or One More for the Road. For Chrissakes, her mother would holler. Sometimes the singing stopped and both their voices, his and hers, went loud. She had the feeling then of things not aligning with how she thought they should be. But if he were to come home she could match them up again. Like shuffling cards before a game of Go Fish then setting them right.

Ask it something, go ahead. Bored, curious, or condescending, her sister had finally agreed to see if, together, they could raise a spirit.

This is silly. You know that, right?

Three weeks now. She was almost ready to give up. But maybe, just maybe, the two of them could make something happen.

Her sister drummed her fingernails on the board, just below where it said Good-Bye.

Anyway, what if you do get an answer? Then what?

She tried to think of a response, one that would make her sound smart. Even after that time at Rite Aid she still thought of him as lost. All he needed was a little coaxing and he'd come home.

Her sister grabbed the planchette and set it in the middle of the board, aiming it at the moon. Where, oh spirit, did our father go? she intoned, exaggerating the final vowel into a ghostly, cartoonish moan.

The planchette jolted.

Look! It's moving! She glanced at her sister as the planchette slid towards the letter "U," pausing there before veering to the "R" and "A," lurching back to the other side of the board, resting at letters, careening wildly, twice settling on the "S" before stopping altogether.

"U" she recited. "R" "A" "D"

U-R-A-D-U-M-B-A-S-S her sister said. Ha! It does know something after all.

* * *

The chocolate cake her mother had made was cooling on the cake stand. In the evening there would be presents, pizza with her choice of topping.

Months since he'd left, a new school year about to start.

Her sister had been right. The Ouija board was just a game, no different than Parcheesi. She'd left it unboxed in the workroom with the other dusty things.

I know what you're doing, her sister had said on her way to the mall with some friends. He's not going to call. You may as well come with us.

But if he did call—which of course he would—suppose she weren't there?

The house was so quiet she could hear the kitchen clock. She spooned peanut butter from the nearly empty jar, ate a fistful of pretzels. In her mother's room she lay across the foot of the bed, staring at the print on the wall, palm trees black against a popsicle sky, the sea silver-flecked. A place at the edge of the world, a place where pirates lived, neon parrots gripping their shoulders. Mermaids, perhaps, their tails submerged so you'd never know. Like her mother at Halloween, her false eyelashes and blonde wig hiding the thing beneath. If only she could stay that way.

A car horn was blaring, startling her from sleep. Her mother in the driveway. She had packages, bags, two plastic sacks in hand, a third balanced on her hip. Saddlebag purse, jailer's ring of keys, a pile of mail that she tossed onto the table.

For you, she said, pointing with her elbow at a hot pink envelope, the name and address in block print. Go ahead and open it if you want.

The handwriting was his all right, the space for the return address left blank. She tore into the envelope. A beaming princess in a glitter crown held a star-tipped wand. Inside were two twenty dollar bills and a printed message: *A birthday greeting on this day, may all you wish for come your way.* He'd signed it Love, Dad.

Well that's just dandy, her mother said. I suppose that's his idea of child support. She snatched one of the bills off the table. One for you, and one for the bank.

No fair! she cried, and her mother said, You're telling me.

After pizza there were presents. A jet bead necklace from her sister and, from her mother, two new sweaters and something unexpected, the earrings she'd seen in the jewelry store window, small silver hoops in a velvet lined box.

We'll go get your ears pierced this weekend, her mother said. You're old enough now, I think.

Make a wish, her sister said.

Twelve pink candles ringed the cake. In yellow icing her mother had written Happy Birthday, the "a" and "y" of Birthday squashed together at the far edge of the cake, the same cake her mother had been making every year for as long as she could remember, with its same wobbly letters and pink frosting roses. Next year there would be thirteen candles and her sister would be old enough to drive. Then her sister would be gone, off to college or a job, a life with new people, and it would be just the two of them until her own turn to leave came and her mother would be left alone to pad around the house in slippers, eating canned soup for dinner, sleeping on weekends as late as she liked.

C'mon already! Her sister scraped a line of frosting off the side of the cake and licked it from her fingernail.

Stop that! her mother said, but she was laughing, her face gone soft. She struck a match and in the glow of the candles she looked younger, nearly pretty, as if the woman she'd once been was still there, just beneath the crinkly mask.

What to wish for? She took a deep breath.

She was not a princess; her mother was not Rapunzel. They lived nowhere near the beach. Try as she might, no spirits would materialize to offer guidance. All they had was right here. For now, at least, it would have to be enough.

She blew out the candles.

Her mother clapped.

I know what you wished for, her sister said, but she would not be goaded into telling. Let her sister believe what she liked; her wish was her own.

For a long time they sat together, the three of them at the table. Their paper plates were frosting smeared, their napkins soiled and wadded, the open pizza box littered with crusts. She felt sated from so much food, sleepy despite her accidental nap. Her mother cut another slice of cake. Who wants more, she asked? Anyone want more?

Vigil

We were in General Math and because the seating was alphabetical, she had a place up front. From the back of the room we could see her, hair shiny with grease, white stripe of skin where her shirt hiked, balding patches on a silver glitter belt. Two at a time she'd fold sticks of gum into her mouth, lips stained dark, eyelids, we knew, caked blue or green. Bangles reached her elbows. Feather earrings tickled her neck.

Our own parents—watchful, conservative—would not send us into the world looking showy. Their word. For us they wanted "better." Homework and curfew, extracurricular activities. We failed tryouts, got walk-ons in plays, skipped band practice and yearbook meetings. We went to the same church, ate dinner at six every day, the same foods: meat loaf, tuna casserole, pork chops with string beans and potatoes. The meals only slightly more palatable versions of cafeteria lunches.

At her house were the foods we craved. Stuffed cabbage, goulash, sutni szalonna. Chicken paprikash, swamped in gravy. People coming, people going, her uncles who spoke no English, a grandmother, tiny and stooped, cousins, the screen door banging, her brother off doing something bad. Her father with his tantrums. He once threw a vacuum cleaner into the street, another time a bowling ball. Her mother, mini-skirted, ice blonde, wailing Why did I marry you, have these brats? And her little sister running around with fingers in her ears crying La La La I love Mickey Mouse!

Serene in the chaos, Janine would lead us upstairs. Her TV on, bed made, pillows just so, drugstore perfumes lined up on the dresser, lip glosses arranged in a semi-circle. Eyelash curler, nail polish, tweezers. A bottle of Nair. We had tried it, smearing the cream on our calves, gagging at the sulphur smell, four pairs of legs in the tub.

Weekends we'd pile on her bed and watch movies on her little TV. *Creature Feature, The Late Show, The 4:30 Movie*, whatever was on, laughing at the fakeness of the mummy or admiring the way Marilyn walked, practicing, getting it wrong. But if one of *his* movies came on, we would not talk. She would not let us.

This was her litany: *The Hustler*, broken hand. *Sweet Bird of Youth*, broken nose. *Cat on a Hot Tin Roof*, broken foot. *Somebody Up There Likes Me*, beat up. *Hud*, beat up. *Cool Hand Luke*, killed. *Butch Cassidy*, killed. *The Left Handed Gun*, killed. Is there anybody in the world that tough?

Her brother, Johnny, thought he was that tough. He had a skull tattoo, cigarettes in his t-shirt sleeve, long black hair, stubble. His jeans were torn and tight. He drove a black Camaro and sometimes after we'd helped with his GED homework he'd drive us home, Janine riding shotgun, each of us hoping to be dropped off last, a block or two away so our parents wouldn't know. Which of you uglies first? he'd tease and we'd all think, secretly, not me. With Janine, he'd tease about other things.

Guess who I saw buying rubbers in the Seven Eleven? Or: You'll never believe who was hitchhiking on Black Rock Turnpike.

Because he knew—we all did—that her idol lived only two towns away.

* * *

We had our own list: Things Borrowed, Not Returned. Money, mostly. And cigarettes. A Led Zeppelin album. A tortoise shell barrette, a red crew-neck sweater, two tubes of hand cream, a pair of socks, a bracelet, a comb, some lipstick we were Not Supposed to Have. We weren't worried, we were just keeping track.

When *The Sting* opened at The Capitol Theatre she borrowed admission. We shared a bucket of popcorn, passed around Cokes. Janine hissed our chewing and when the credits rolled she hid in the ladies' room. She would sneak or bluff or cajole her way back in, she didn't care, were we staying? We were not. The movie, with its old-fashioned music, its poker and cigars, had bored us. Besides, we had to go home.

Twice! she gloated the next afternoon. Piece of cake, I can't believe you didn't stay. She'd return that night, she swore, if she didn't have to babysit her sister who was, just then, running around naked while her mother screamed Get back here you God damned brat and her father sang drunkenly in his foreign tongue.

We'd come by to do something, we didn't care what. Saturday, the chores done, the whole long day to kill.

Janine sat cross-legged on the floor. She'd lit patchouli against the rising smell of cabbage. Incense smoldered in bedside burners, candles smoked a choking perfume. Only those and the TV gave off light. She'd been decorating. Glossy photos of his face were crammed into the mirror frame. Some were pasted directly onto the glass. Scattered on the floor were magazines, *TV Guides*, glue sticks, highlighters, wadded napkins, plates of sandwich crusts, cups and glasses varnished with residue.

Downstairs, her father's singing surged. Her mother shrieked in response. The sister wailed. Something hit the wall and shattered. We heard footsteps, hard on the stairs. The candle flames shook. Janine jumped up to lock the door, too late.

Jesus Christ what the fuck are they fighting about now wait till they find out I flunked the GED again...You!

Johnny flopped across the bed. He smiled at us, not friendly. Some God damn help you all were.

Take your feet off my bed.

Johnny sat up. He lit a cigarette. Janine asked for one and he showed her the empty pack. Then he crumpled it, tossed it into the mess. Dust bunnies rose and settled.

Let's get the hell out of here, he said.

We did not ask. It was enough to be going somewhere. Late afternoon, the vacancy sign switched on, the big neon letters of the Bridgeport Motor Inn burnt out in places—a T, an R—so the sign read Bridgeport Mo o Inn, which made Johnny laugh.

Moo Inn, that's about right for you cows. He parked across the street, cut the engine and turned to us, hunched as always in the back seat. No talking. Got it?

We followed him through the empty lot. He kicked at leftover snow. Our sneakers scraped gravel. Quiet! he whispered, so we tiptoed, except Janine, sockless and silent in clogs. She blew on her fingers—so many rings!—and stayed close to Johnny.

He led us through a back door into the room with the vending machines. Slumped beside the lobby phone, right around the corner, the desk clerk slept, white-haired, snoring, older than we could ever imagine being and living out his days at the Bridgeport Motor Inn.

Johnny touched his finger to his lips, a little boy gesture, sweet. He cracked his knuckles. The vending machines, the stained orange carpet, the improbable paintings of clouds and clipper ships, everything in that small room seemed to hum.

Watch this, Johnny mouthed. Legs splayed, he pressed his hands against the sides of the cigarette machine and began to rock it, gently, taking small steps backwards, bending his knees, bringing the machine closer and closer to his chest. Packs of cigarettes tumbled out. Then coins, a trickle, a stream. Johnny rocked and rocked. The machine gave up its bounty. When he finished, we poured coins into his hands.

Now you. He pointed at the candy machine.

Janine had filled her purse with cigarettes. She set it on top of the ice chest and began to riffle through it for gum. We glanced at each other, at Janine, her back to us, at Johnny, grinning a threat. With its rows and rows of chocolate bars, the candy machine looked heavier, somehow, than its flimsy counterpart, the cigarette machine.

We waited.

Jesus Christ! Janine said. All right.

Not you. Them.

She shrugged and hitched herself onto the ice chest. There was nothing left to do. One by one we took up her brother's challenge. Johnny and Janine watched our shoulders rise as we inhaled, warming up, watched us, in turn, grab the machine the way Johnny had, pulling at it, panting, our knees flexed, our faces turning red, cheeks puffing with effort, neck cords bulging.

Muscle! Johnny grunted. Put some muscle into it! But chocolates, mints, caramels stayed fixed in their orbits.

Janine swung her legs. She snapped her gum. This is stupid, she said. They're not like that.

Like what? Johnny held up his hand, signal to stop. He swaggered over to us, solid, a machine himself, looking like he would just lift that candy machine over his head and carry it to the car.

Dumb fucks! Look. It's bolted to the wall. How fuckin' stupid can you be?

Nearly helpless with laughter, Janine was holding onto her stomach as if to keep from falling off the ice chest. So, she gasped, who flunked the GED?

She stopped coming to school. We heard pneumonia, mono, influenza, something, anyway, requiring quarantine and long convalescence. We imagined her, small under quilts, spooning her mother's healing concoctions, sipping strange teas, luxuriating in the syrup of game shows, soap operas, sitcom reruns.

The girl we saw, we finally saw, was a figurine, chalk-boned, shrunken, her eyes glassy from (she confessed) staying up all night, watching his movies or working on The Book. This was her project, all consuming, a scrapbook of every photo, fact, and film clip, a life at her fingertips.

She'd come to school late, leave early, barely speak to anyone, an apparition in rumpled clothes, ancient chips of polish on her nails, scalp powdered with dry shampoo.

Come to the mall, we'd say. Come to the movies, the park. But no, she could never, she would not.

More rumors. She was flunking all her classes. The truant officer had come to her home. She was being suspended, grounded, her parents were divorcing, she was taking GED classes with Johnny. In Math, her seat was empty.

We stopped asking. We understood. Illness was a sanctuary. Alone in her room, she was keeping vigil.

Summer we took on disposable jobs. We got learners' permits, drove to the beach. Oil-slicked, we sprawled on thin towels, brushed sand from arms, legs, rubbed lotion into each other's backs, our skin freckled, burnt, tanned, or peeling. We sang along to crackling ballads about perfect love, endless love, fraught love, unrequited love, thinking, perhaps, that we knew.

Rainy days we headed for the mall, where the earrings sparkled and the shoes were so much richer with possibility than our Dr. Scholl's.

Janine! We conjured her. Locked in her room, lost to summer, she'd grown huge, barely able to waddle downstairs. Or she was wasting away, a stick in the dark, hair caked white. Once we thought we saw her, trying on belts at Bradlees, but it was another girl, older, with acne on her forehead and a t-shirt from Wesleyan. The girl, a disappointment, looked at us blandly. A blue-smocked clerk paused in her pricing, said May I Help...then stopped. She'd heard—or felt—the strange buzzing, an electric current of voices. People were massing at its source.

Girls! A smocked saleswoman yelped. Girls, did you hear? Paul Newman's in the store.

And then we saw him, pushing a shopping cart of gardening utensils, a middle-aged man, smaller than his movie self. People gaped. We gaped. A woman ran towards him, waving a scrap of paper. He signed it and the entire store swarmed, a frenzy of salesclerks, housewives, toddlers dragged by the hand, gawky boys, giggling girls, even a couple of grown men. All of Bradlees tried to touch him, talk to him, get his autograph. With his cart he fended them off, pushing ahead, but we stood dumbly in the aisle, blocking his way.

Girls? he said. Starstruck, stupid, we began snatching at things. A cardboard box of pantyhose, a magazine, a paperback. Aren't you a little young he joked, signing his name to the cover of *The Joy of Sex*.

Later we cursed our muteness. We invented scenarios, repartee, witty comebacks that led to conversation. Later, smoking cigarettes, reliving the event, we got it right. But we had something, anyway. We had his autograph.

It was more than she had.

We wanted to tell her, show her, make her repent her isolation. For a while we even thought we would.

Poinsettias

She folded inward where she'd made the cut, a neat seam to hide the ragged edge. Heavy gold paper printed with poinsettias, she did not remember buying it. She'd found the roll, sheathed in dusty plastic, at the back of the bedroom closet the morning she'd packed his shoes for Goodwill.

All day the radio had been playing carols: *Peace on Earth, Good Will To Men; Oh Come, All Ye Faithful.* His station, the oldies one. She'd not bothered to change it, though it was classical she preferred.

The paper was slightly garish, in the way of poinsettias. One year he'd filled the back seat with them—a surprise! They'd banked white ones on the hutch, red ones for a centerpiece, oblivious to danger until she'd caught the cat on the table, chewing away, then puking up red and howling as if to die. She'd tossed the dammed things out, all of them, just to be safe. Holly berries, Christmas rose, bleeding heart, snow drops, too many things to name, nature's pretties harboring secret poison.

Wrapping gifts felt easy enough, a small mechanical act. Bring the edges together, smooth any lumps. Rampant flowers like a woman's summer skirt. One piece of tape, precisely in the center. Alone, she'd ceased to care about appearances, wore gym shorts, a man's oversized t-shirt, one of several she'd kept. Souvenir shirts bought for laughs: the Leaning Tower, pyramids, Big Ben. The radiator clanged and hissed. She'd opened windows to let out the massed heat—other people's stoves and lamps and microwaves, everyone clustered together in this big new complex, cells in a hive.

Baby, it's cold outside, a man sang, cajoling his date into lingering, melting her no to yes with cocktails and cigarettes, small pleasures she'd given up in support. She'd not missed them and the not missing had been an unexpected balm.

Roll out more paper, start a new box. Bottles for the grownups— his siblings, hers—and for their children books and sweaters, things easily exchanged. A failure of imagination, she supposed, but she was at a loss. What did they want, children? Having none, it was difficult to say. They'd tried at first, with thermometers and charts, all that fussing over calendars. Briefly, too, they'd considered adoption, but the cost, the uncertainty, and besides, he'd said, you're the only one I really want. So there'd been late mornings with the papers, restaurants, vacations, tombs and ruins—Egypt, Mexico—and for her the gardens of Italy, England, France. Commiserating over the phone with some sleep deprived friend, she'd been careful to conceal her relief.

Had they noticed it anyway, her friends, some slight smugness on her part? Later, when it was their turn to listen, she could not bring herself to speak. Ministering with soup, casseroles, anodyne clichés. Time and wounds, move on, move past, past pain, beyond and yonder... words to pain her head. Words! How foolish once to have been in their sway. And how impotent now, changing nothing.

Midnight she would go to mass, take twice-a-year communion, the host, the wine, body and blood. He'd had none of that, teasing her about holiday Catholics. *No mumbo jumbo for me, you make certain.* Which of course she did, forsaking ritual for an urn and some unscripted words spoken by whoever cared, then good stiff drinks, the first she'd had in ages.

Unspool ribbon, white satin or the red one for curling. No need to rush. Measure and tie, curl the ends with scissors. Trim loose pieces and scraps, stray bits of hair, toenails. Measure liquid into spoons, spoon into glasses, measure the hours in between. Measure lotion into palms, soothe into sores, powder heavily, shocked at how loose the pajamas have become. Buy new pajamas, a sporty new hat, sports shirts, items

obtained on credit, to be paid for at some future date. Wrap in tissue
and ribbon, a surprise. Toss out pajamas, hats, and shirts. Toss shoes,
rugs, mirrors, the too large bed, its blankets and sheets. So many boxes
the Goodwill had sent men. Photos she kept, his gifts and cards, the
ring she now wore, awkwardly-sized to fit the middle finger of her left
hand, so that it clicked against her own plain band.

Let go she had been told, as if that were not simple. Drinks, meals,
cigarettes. Muscle and fat. The morning she'd glimpsed herself, wet
from the shower, a tangle of hair, an outcropping of bones—ribs,
clavicles—those ribbony tendons in her neck. She'd gone for the scissors, black lumps furring the white tiles. She would have a monk's
head, tonsured and gray. Afterwards she'd wandered from room to
room, starting at the sound of her voice when she realized, abruptly,
that she'd been speaking aloud, giving herself gentle guidance: *We
must finish folding sheets. We must pack one more box.*

Friends, too, that was easy enough. Telling her you must get out,
scheduling lunches against a backdrop of blaring televisions, barking
dogs, other people's demands—*Hold on!* and *Where was I?* Not their
fault, of course, but she'd had to stop taking the calls.

Memories were trickier because there were things she wanted to
retain. Anniversaries, holidays, martinis on the deck, steaks grilled
too rare though she never complained, his goofy striped apron, the
time in Baja she'd swum too far, an undertow, and he'd pulled her
back. Shivering while he hollered, enraged at her carelessness. *You
almost drowned!* His hands on her shoulders, the strength of him. *I
could have lost you!* And been left alone to cope. How often she'd
thought that, thought of the water's pull, gentle at first, through all
the days she'd learned to be careful.

Whatever routine bickering they'd endured, surely some. Whose
idea it had been to give up first, to give up altogether. No longer young,
he'd reminded her of that, reminded her of the difference in their ages,
the paperwork involved, home visitors with their questions, how long
it all would take. *It wouldn't be ours, not really, and besides, I only want
you.*

On the table a strip of candy canes. She snipped one loose, removed it from its wrapper. With curling ribbon she fastened it to a bow. Such order and symmetry in the patterned stripes, red on white, nothing out of balance, the one overtaking the other, a mass of cells, a host of words—*lymphocyte, anemia, autoimmunity*—those ugly crowded vowels.

Soon she would shower, dress, go to mass.

In the morning she would take the boxes down, load the trunk, make the drive. She told herself that. The children eager, tearing at paper, while their parents, sweetly sleepy, buzzed on Bloody Marys, kept watch. Scraps of gift wrap, pistachio shells in cushions, wet rings on tables, a dog running through legs, an afternoon of drinks, gifts, good will. What could they possibly give her?

That time she'd been convinced, but it was nothing. She'd been late was all.

A church bell rang the hour. She put her scissors down.

She rose early, loaded the car, pausing to pick lint from the folds of her skirt. She was expected somewhere. Instead, she drove to the familiar house, their house, made strange with lawn angels and colored lights. For a while she idled there, though pressed, she could not have said why. She watched the colored lights blink, watched shapes move behind the picture window, watched her hands on the wheel as she moved back into traffic. She drove over bridges and ramps, past scattered houses, drove with the visor down against the slanted sun. So much land. The sky turned pale then dark, and still she kept driving until the road emptied into a field of icy stubble that crunched underfoot. Ice soaked the leather of her dress pumps, numbing her toes. The moon, a waning sliver, barely lit her way. Where she was headed she did not know except that it was a clear, cold, empty place, far from anywhere she had been before.

Hold On Fast

He came dripping from the sea, seaweed caught in his yellow hair. His towel—plaid, ordinary—separate from our blanket, the one with the lipstick kiss pattern. The lips were a joke, but he did not think so, one more stupid thing. Shook his head, hair flying, water spraying my stomach and arms. If you asked him for money for a hotdog or Coke he'd say get lost. If you asked for a cigarette he'd make you ask twice. We'd squint at the sea and smoke.

The transistor buzzed bright tinny songs about the wonders of love. Horseshit! he said, throwing the radio down in the sand.

Twerps. He called us that and hags and Dismal Debbies which made me think of those cupcakes—Little Debbies—with their swirls of hard white frosting.

What the hell's so funny, he'd say. Bunch of loons.

A loon's a bird.

Yeah. And you're a birdbrain.

He made us sit in back because what if his friends were to see. Two girls, both in junior high, one of them his kid sister. The only way his mother would let him take her car: If you're just going alone, you can bring your sister, too. How selfish can you be?

He'd drop her early at work, pick her up late at her second job.
Their father gone, who could say where, we had the run of the place.
James, we called him, pretending he was our chauffeur. James, take
us for a spin.

Because he loved water—Correction, he said, the beach, I love the
beach—because he loved the beach, he'd chosen a college in Florida.
A scholarship, a smart kid. Could've gone Ivy, his mother complained—which you could've fooled me. Because he loved water
you'd think he'd have majored in something aquatic, marine biology
or oceanography or something like that, but he claimed there was
plenty of time. Besides, he *was* studying the local marine life. His
hands made hourglass curves in the air. We were sticks with frizzed
out hair and skin that peeled and nothing much to show. We knew
that. He didn't have to rub it in.

In her bureau mirror we practiced glamour. Smeared on eye
shadow, green and blue, that we'd stolen from Caldor's. Practiced tying
our shirttails into knots. We stuffed tissue into our bras, smoothing
them, trying to get it right. He teased us about this, hooting with
laughter. Lopsided Lunatics. How do you know? we asked and he
looked at me and said, You were standing right by the window. She
was furious. What were you doing looking? I could feel myself
redden.

We smelled it in the den, a sweet smell when he thought no one
was home. Give us, we said. Let us try. Give us and we won't make
you take us to the mall.
    He said we were too young. His sister picked up his glasses from the
coffee table. She twisted her thick dark hair into a bun. With the

glasses and the bun she looked like a TV librarian. Mom, she said.
Mom, I have something to tell you. It's about James…
Okay, okay. You win. He was laughing and he tossed the baggie on
the table.

He showed us how to roll a skinny one with the papers he'd got at
Dynamite Dave's where everyone went to buy records. His were
Black Sabbath, Blue Öyster Cult, Deep Purple. He played them in
the den, songs about death and fire and iron. When the joint came
my way I exhaled fast like with a cigarette. Hold it, he said. Don't
blow it back out, you stupid twerp.

Next time I did like he said, holding the smoke till I almost
couldn't breathe. I coughed and coughed. He patted my back. The
song was going Shake it, shake it, girl, and I thought about milk-
shakes, how sweet they were, how they could make your teeth ache,
sweetly, and suddenly I wanted one.

We made a summer of pestering him. Trailed him to the beach
whenever he didn't have a "client," his fancy word for the people whose
lawns he mowed. His friends called us jailbait. They shared their weed.
One of them sat close to me, his arm on the back of the couch.

Go rinse that shit off your face, James said. You look like a clown.

When I came back he was on the couch and I had to sit on the
floor.

His hand, touching mine, passing the joint, not pulling away.

The music was men telling women to lie down. Or shake it. Sometimes there were noises like machines.

For a joke we switched records, putting one of hers in the sleeve
for *Dark Side of the Moon*. It took him a while to realize. Elton John

was singing "Sweet Painted Lady" to a background of seagulls. There
was a shriek and the needle scudded over vinyl. We barely had time
to lock the bedroom door. The record smashed against it and later we
threw the jagged pieces into the trash.

He started letting me ride up front. His sister said no fair, take
turns, but he ignored her.

We were practicing with the curling iron, making our hair go flat.
The bathroom smelled of fried hair and raspberry lip gloss. You could
be Cher, she told me. You could be Cher if your hair were longer.
And black instead of brown. And maybe if you were taller.

The car was a stick shift. He let me sit up front and showed me the
gears, his hand over mine: First, second, reverse. See? Automatics are
for pussies.

End of summer he came home late. We were in the den watching
Don Kirshner's Rock Concert. His pupils huge and the way he walked,
stiff-legged, scuffing his feet. Stoned, we said. You are so stoned. His
face said nothing. He stared at the lines in his palm, curling his fingers inward, then straightening them in slow motion. He did this
again and again. We left him there, sitting in the den, tracing the
lines in his palm.

The next day he was normal. He even offered to drop us at the
mall on his way to work.

What we found in his room: *Playboys*, E-Z Widers, some dirty
glasses and mugs. Condoms! We found a dried up orange rind. We

found a baggie that was mostly seed and a vial with some tiny purple pills. We shook them in the vial. It sounded like maracas.

Then we didn't see him. He kept his door locked. The days were yellow and blue. We knocked and yelled, James. It's a beach day, James, come out. The door opened, just a crack. Like peering at a slide through a view finder, aiming your eye towards the light. The shades drawn, one little nightlight glowing against the wall. He wore padded headphones. Touched his finger to his lips and shut the door.

We began calling him Boo. From the lawn we chanted up to him. Boo Radley Boo Radley, let down your long hair. Girls! their mother cried. Girls, aren't you ashamed? She drove herself to work so there was no more car.

He was packing, his door open, shades up, music loud. School was starting for everyone. We sat in the kitchen eating cheese sandwiches and making lists. What we needed: jeans, boots with cowboy stitching, hoop earrings, Danskins. How much we'd saved over the summer babysitting (not much). How much (the earrings, some lipsticks) we figured we could steal.

We'd made a pact to ignore him because look at the weirdo he'd become. Secretly, though, I wanted to say good-bye. My back was to the room and I kept twisting around in my chair.

Quit it, she said.

What?

If you want to go see him just go.

Maybe I will, I said, but instead I went to think things over while I peed. His laundry was stacked on the dryer in the little bathroom off the kitchen. I picked up a t-shirt, still warm, pressed it to my cheek. It smelled like laundry. I flipped it open, a flamingo, a palm tree.

The door handle shook.

All right all right all right, I yelled. She was bugging me way too much. I'd decided to go home. Quickly I balled the shirt into my jeans, letting my shirttails hang loose.

Took you long enough.

I looked past him into the empty kitchen.

I'm going home, I said. Good luck in Florida.

Good luck in Flor-i-da. What're you, a Hallmark card?

He stood there blocking my path. His t-shirt felt hot against my stomach.

Well? he said. I tried to think of something smart. He'd lost his tan, his skin ghostly, hair shiny with grease like maybe he'd forgotten about showers. Light from the prism mobile in the bathroom window made rainbows on the wall above his head. Soon he'd be in Florida with the bathing beauties and I'd be in Algebra I.

When he put his hand on my shoulder, I thought he'd seen the bulge under my shirt. But he wasn't looking there. He was looking at me.

You're all right, he said. For a pain in the ass. He kissed my forehead, like a priest, then my mouth, like a boy. It was over before I could shut my eyes.

Move it, he said. I gotta pack.

Christmas he came home for a month. I had school, couldn't go out on weeknights. The weekend of the blizzard, though, I got stuck at her house. We wore pajamas and made popcorn and watched whatever was on TV: Elvis Presley in Hawaii, reruns of *Bewitched* and *Twilight Zone*.

His room was above the den and I kept listening for sounds: footsteps, music, anything. I knew he was home, she'd told me so, but she'd also told me he never left his room, not even to eat. It was driving their mother nuts.

I tried to picture him lying in bed, headphones on, or sitting at his desk, maybe sneaking into the kitchen for a bowl of cereal when everyone was asleep. Like a monk with heavy metal music instead of prayer.

Late that night, early morning, I didn't know, I woke up from the cold. The blanket had slid from the sleeper couch to the floor. It was still snowing hard, the sky stained glass purple. I got some water and drank it by the living room window, a girl half awake in borrowed pajamas, watching snow make the familiar world disappear.

Something moved.

At first I thought I imagined it, the sweep of arms on the ground. But no, it was him—James, Boo—making angels in the snow. He wore a t-shirt, boxers, his head and feet bare. A streetlight shone on his deep, curved wings. His face in darkness, impossible to say what he felt.

I wanted him to stop. I wanted to bring him a coat. We're not angels, I wanted to say. The world filled up with snow, his arms and legs pushing it away.

You won't believe it, she said. You better come see.

His hair was shaved into uneven yellow bristles. Patches of scalp showed through. Creased khakis, a white shirt buttoned to his throat. The buzz cut made him beaky. Five months since I'd seen him that night in the snow. I never told. It was a secret between us, only he didn't know.

Reborn, he said. He'd been reborn.

Reborn into what, I wondered. This new boy—not James, not Boo, someone we had no name for—read the Bible in the den. At meals he said grace. His mother rolled her eyes and folded her hands. We kept our hands in our laps. Brainwashed, we told each other. We thought up ways to deprogram him. Hypnosis, loud music, field trips to Dynamite Dave's. He went nowhere, saw no one, just him and Jesus in the den.

I thought I knew about Jesus. He turned water into wine and hung out with Mary Magdalene. Not this Jesus though. This Jesus wanted your pain. Do as he says or you're going to hell. Did we know how hot hell was? What torment awaited us there? Look!

On the table was a Bic lighter. With his thumb he spun the little dial that controlled the flame so the flame went shooting up.

Touch it, he dared. Go ahead.

He held the flame under my hand. I made a fist. The flame wavered beneath my knuckles. We stared at each other, a game of chicken. His eyes behind his glasses were the hard bright eyes of a doll. He brought the flame closer and I let out a little yelp and pulled my hand away.

You see? he said.

He was dropping us at the movies, a matinee. Because she couldn't find her wallet we were running late. He drove slowly, the way he did everything now.

C'mon! we said. At least go the speed limit.

Listen, he said, and turned up the volume on the radio. Listen, this is the greatest love song ever. He began singing along with Barry Manilow about angels and cyclones and stallions. Could it be magic? he sang in his off-kilter voice.

We came to a stop sign. In the back seat we looked at each other, amazed.

Quit it, we yelled. Let's go! But he did not go. He cranked the volume so high the windows vibrated and we had to put our fingers in our ears.

Cars honked. Drivers drove around us, shot us the bird. When the song ended, it felt like we'd escaped something.

The day he started the fire was drizzly, which should tell you something, I guess, someone trying to burn things in the rain. Barefoot we ran outside, the grass spongy and cold. He'd dug a pit in the back yard and the fire was in there, more smoke than flames.

All sorts of things were heaped on the ground: t-shirts, paper-backs, *Mad* magazines, a bong, the *Playboys* we'd discovered.

One by one he was ripping out centerfolds. Miss April, Miss May, who knew which months, he crumpled them into the pit. So much smoke my eyes stung. We ran in circles, hollering. Like a steam shovel he kept at it, scooping things up, dumping them down. His glasses filmed with rain. The fire was barely a fire. She grabbed him from behind and he pushed her so that she went stumbling into a stack of books. Here! she shrieked, kicking them into the fire. Here, burn the whole fuckin' house down, why don't you?

The pages smoldered and caught. Beside me she stood crying, shivering in the drizzle.

Mud and ashes and smoke, books charred or soaked so they'd dry, if they dried, swollen and unreadable. This was what he had made. The magazines were pulp: torsos and cars and liquor ads all stuck together. He turned his back on this ruin, the scraps of his life, and returned to the house. The flames were spreading, paper fed.

He came back wearing his denim jacket and cradling something to his chest. Whatever it was was going next; he wouldn't stop until all of it, every last shred, was consumed, all the books and clothes and furniture, the feelings and ideas, anything that had once been him, and the sound I made—that single NO!—startled me as he opened his arms wide, releasing his records.

Done. It was the only word he said. The screen door slammed behind him.

She was the one who reached in first. We pulled out as many as we could and spread them on the lawn. Some of the records looked all right. Some of them were warped. We thought maybe we could save them, roll them flat, reshape them somehow. We thought we could make them play again.

In My Solitude

Songs

After my mother grew fat, my father left her for a frosted blonde named Doris. This was the summer before I entered sixth grade. Sundays, I visited him at Doris's apartment, where he was staying. With its pool, its mauve hallway carpet, its soda and snack machines, her apartment complex resembled a motel. We'd drag three chaise lounges to the pool's edge. Doris, in paisley bikini and hot pink sunglasses, would sun herself while my father read the paper and I practiced diving.

Andrea, she would yell, sitting up, crimson nails raking silvered hair. Don't splash!

But I'd already be at the shallow end.

It took Doris days to rearrange herself, adjusting sunglasses, reapplying lotion, raising and lowering the chaise lounge, finally, inevitably, flopping onto her stomach. My father would massage her back with tanning oil, kneading the muscles the same way he'd later marinate chicken pieces for the grill.

Worcestershire sauce, Tobasco, lemon juice, salt—just a pinch—pay attention, honey. He enunciated each ingredient as if he himself were responsible for its existence. Sang, rubbing garlic into veiny meat, swirling chicken breasts in dark sauce.

Am I blue, wouldn't you be, too . . .

One sad song followed another. Doris, fresh from the shower, would wander into the kitchen, robed in terry cloth, turbaned, white circles around her eyes from the sunglasses. She had a face like an egg salad sandwich.

Standing over the grill my father would sing:

I ain't got nobody, nobody cares for me...

No one, I thought, had the right to seem so happy.

Home

It was nothing like Doris's apartment. At home, we ate takeout from cuisine specific places: one for chicken, another for fish, places for pizza, hamburgers. Or frozen meals, readymade and lurid. Peas in yellow sauce. Orange tacos. I liked them better than my father's food.

My mother was growing huge. She wore stretch pants and printed shirts from Large 'n Luscious. Little white socks. Even her feet were fat, flesh spilling over the sides of her doll-like shoes. She took a job as hot lunch lady, spooning mashed potatoes, runny meatloaf, creamed corn onto plastic plates. Her upper lip sweaty, her hair in a net. Fatso Buttso, the other kids called her. Hey Andrea, I saw your mother at the circus. She was trying on tents.

I hated school, all that lining up for buses, for bathrooms, and food. The dusty warm taste of cafeteria milk and the way my teacher's arm jiggled when she wrote on the board. Most of all I hated thinking about my mother.

New York

Summer fall winter spring enough was enough, he said. She wanted too much, he said. Doris is a nice lady, don't get me wrong.

Saturday mornings my father drove in from the city. He'd pull into our driveway, honk the horn and Hold it! my mother would say. He could have the decency to get out of that car.

She wanted him to bring me home on Sundays; he said it was too much driving. Twice he refused to make the trip. It was my mother who relented. I could take the train home provided my father himself put me on said train then waited on the platform until it left the station. He agreed to buy my ticket, too.

My father's new home was a basement on the Upper East Side. I would peek through the window bars at passersby, their sneakers and dress shoes, their clumpy little dogs. If I tilted my head back far enough, I could see a slice of sky wedged between two buildings. My bed was a pullout couch. The kitchen was inside a closet: mini fridge, two burners, toaster oven, cupboard. Mostly we ate out.

We went to Chinatown where the pay phones, nestled into pagodas, made me wish I had someone to call. We saw The Dancing Chicken! It was in a red wooden box outside a Chinese restaurant. The box had wire mesh across the top, a peep window and a coin slot. Fifty cents caused tinny hoe-down music to play from hidden speakers. A yellow bulb lit up; tiny marquee lights flashed around the window. Like a chorus girl the chicken came strutting from behind a curtain and did its dance, neck bobbing, feet scratching, all out of sync with the music. Two minutes, three, some feed slid down a chute into a bowl and the lights switched off, end of show.

I felt sorry for the chicken, stuck inside that box. I wondered whether it was the same chicken each time or if they had different ones. What happened if the chicken got tired? Did it wind up in the lo mein? But my father would laugh and laugh—Look at that chicken go! And then I would laugh, too.

He took me to street fairs in Little Italy, the air thick with odors: sausage grease, charcoal fumes, garlic, hot peppers, fried dough; our plates damp and heavy as we strolled beneath strings of colored lights, my father letting me sip from his cup of Chianti—Don't tell your mother. We had to shout over the broadcast blare of festival music. I liked it because we didn't have to talk.

Often one of my father's girlfriends would join us, a procession of Tinas or Bettys or Debbies, stewardesses or secretaries, thin women who lived alone or maybe with a cat. We'd ride around, my father driving one-handed, elbow out the window, and if one of the Tinas wasn't along, muttering: Hello, Sweetheart! Christ, will you look at that! Turning up the radio, singing In My Solitude. I was always a little afraid he would forget me, leave me behind in Central Park or on the Circle Line Ferry. I kept my eye on him.

But the train! The train was my favorite part. Staring out the scratched window at the blur of receding stations, I could be anyone, going anywhere. All week long I looked forward to that magic hour when I was suspended between worlds, no one to claim me.

Flesh

I stopped eating. I don't know why. It wasn't as if I hated food, but somehow it started to upset me. The way there was so much of it. Every time I turned on the TV. And all that stuff my mother kept in the house—the boxes and bags of chips and candies, cakes and pies crowding the cupboards.

I asked her to buy me some celery sticks. I told her I was eating big lunches. I told her it was my period coming on and she smiled and said I know, I was the same way, and that frightened me. I didn't know what to tell my father.

Look at you. All you ever want is salad.

I just don't feel like eating is all.

Whoever heard of not eating? Besides, you're a beanpole. Built like me. You need to keep up your stamina.

We were at South Street Seaport with one of the Tinas. Gulls circled and squawked, dive bombing the pavement for fish scraps. The air reeked of low tide.

My father tapped my shoulder.

See that? He pointed away from the water, the ravaging gulls, to a cluster of glass towers. That building over there? That's where your father works. That building runs the world.

I couldn't tell which building he meant. My father's job had something to do with insurance, that much I knew. He seemed to be waiting for a response so I shaded my eyes, squinting in a parody of concentration.

It's big, I said. He didn't answer. The day was hot, cloudless, the sun glinting off water, off glass and concrete. Seagulls kept swooping, pecking away at bits of fish—livers, lungs, who knew what else? I began to feel faint.

You look pale, Tina said. Norman, she looks pale.

She needs to eat. Sweetheart, you need to eat.

But I didn't want to eat.

Nonsense, my father said. He led us to a takeout stand where a man was prying open clams and piling them into little paper trays. My father ordered three; the man added a lemon wedge and some cocktail sauce to each tray.

Cherrystones, my father said. He sucked one down.

I considered the mound of grayish-white clams. They're not cooked, I said.

My father laughed and I glanced at Tina for support, but she was eating, too, making small noises of satisfaction. The clams were clots of mucous. I knew I couldn't eat them.

Go on, my father said. Try one. He had stopped laughing.

No, thank you.

Listen, he said, this not eating stuff may work with your mother, but not with me.

I'm not hungry.

I didn't ask if you were.

I'll get sick.

I doubt it. Eat.

With my cocktail fork, I poked at one of the smaller clams. It gave way, gelatinous, an eyeball.

Eat, he ordered.

I pulled the clam from its shell, doused it with lemon juice and sauce, shut my eyes as I guided the offending creature toward my mouth. What if it moved? I tried to swallow it whole, but my throat closed, I tasted metal and, gagging, spat the clam out. It landed near Tina's foot. She shrieked.

That's it, my father said. Get in the car.

We rode in silence. The air felt good on my face. God damned spoiled, my father grumbled and I wished he would put on the radio.

He drove to a part of town I'd never seen before. Men crouched in doorways, swigged from paper bags, some had passed out right there on the sidewalk. The clothes they wore were torn, dirty, too big or too small, uniform in their shabbiness. They were damaged looking, these men, and the buildings they leaned against were damaged, too, with broken or boarded windows, graffiti scrawled walls. We stopped for a light and a bare-chested man in an open blazer came lurching towards us.

Damn it Norman, Tina said. Why didn't you just take the FDR Drive?

Well, he answered, I guess they've gotta live, too.

The man began wiping our windshield with a squeegee, his face close to the glass. He had blotchy skin, a sore above his lip. I looked away.

My father turned around, handed me a dollar. Here, he said. Roll down your window and give it to him.

Norman...Tina said.

No. She needs to learn how other people live. Thinks everything is pick and choose.

The man approached my father.

Give him the money or you can get out and walk.

Norman, for Chrissakes!

My father unlocked my door. Well? You want to stay in this car? The light had turned green; people were honking. I traced a patch of sunlight on the vinyl seat, wishing the man, my father, Tina, all of us would simply disappear. She's got your money, my father said. I unrolled my window, just enough for the man to reach in. His fist closed around the dollar, our fingers almost touching. I let go. The light turned red and we drove off.

That was completely unnecessary, Tina said. You can drop me home.

Fine, he said. Fine. Thinks everything is blue skies and honey. Three meals a day that you can say yes or no to. Your mother lets you get away with murder.

I re-locked my door, huddled against it, trying to make myself small.

My father glanced over his shoulder.

Jesus H. Christ, he bellowed. I was joking. It was a joke. His face relaxed, the anger deflating. Did you *really* think I'd do that?

Waiting Room

They must have made up because the next day Tina was back. My father was treating us to dinner at a hotel restaurant. I had decided to let him order, eat whatever appeared on my plate. And I did manage one or two bites of steak—medium rare—before the pink juices, so close to blood, seeped into my potatoes. So I came up with a plan.

Excuse me, I said and took my plate to the salad bar. Certain that no one was looking, I dumped steak pieces into the vat of blue cheese dressing and loaded up on lettuce. I did this twice. My father and Tina were busy devouring their dinners. Every once in a while my father glanced at his watch. Plenty of time, he'd say, meaning before he had to take me to Grand Central and personally put me on the train as he'd promised to do. And we'd have made it, too, if it weren't for what happened in the lobby, the siren lure of piano music beckoning my father from the hotel bar.

Just one nightcap, he said. We've got half an hour, easy. Tina and I trailed him into the bar. Sit over there, he said, indicating a small table in a dim corner. Order me a scotch and soda. He gave Tina a twenty, went over to the piano and put a bill in the brandy snifter on the piano lid. The piano player looked up. My father said something. The pianist struck a cord, and my father began to sing:

Everybody loves somebody sometime . . .

He had the moves, the sway, even his slicked-back hair looked suddenly right. One song segued into the next, polite applause marking each transition. I speared the cherry in my Coke, banged it against my ice cubes. And that's when I spotted her, this enormous woman in a tight red dress, making her way to her table from the ladies' room. Please just please just please don't let him see her, I prayed, but it was too late. My father, grinning, had gone up-tempo:

It's a ring-a-ding world...
Hey sweetheart
Lovin' wonderful you
Have another donut!

The woman gave him a look like she might just deck him and for a moment I hoped she would. But she kept walking. I stood up.

Okay, okay, my father said, approaching our table. I get the hint. He took a swig of scotch and soda. Listen, honey, he said to Tina, it's early still. You wait here, order another drink. I'll be back in twenty minutes. He kissed her forehead. Half an hour tops.

They loved me in there, he kept repeating in the cab. You hear that applause? I was barely warmed up. Your old man was on a roll, huh?

What time is it?

You'll make it, don't worry. Only look at that line! It'll take me forever to get another cab. She'll be furious. She being Tina, I supposed.

We'd pulled up to the station. The taxi queue stretched to the corner and around the block. I knew what was coming.

My father took out his wallet. You're a big girl now, right sweetheart? he said. You know what to do. Just look at the board for the track number. The New Haven line, the red one. Here, buy your ticket on the train. Call me when you get home so I won't be worried.

I took the money and went tearing into the station. On the announcement board, next to my train, was the word Departed. The hours and minutes began to rearrange themselves, little squares clicking as the numbers flipped. When they finished, I saw that the next train was not for two hours.

I stood there trying to decide what to do. All around me people were running to catch trains, waving to each other, checking the board. They each had somewhere to go. I had somewhere to go, too, even if it wasn't exactly where I wanted to be.

In the concourse I found a bank of phones, asked the operator to place the call collect. An old man walked towards me, his hand open, gaps where his teeth must once have been. I turned my back, pretended to be talking. The man began checking nearby phones for change. Other men, women too, slept bundled on benches, riffled through trash cans, or just sat staring at nothing. They were people who belonged to no one.

My mother came on the line.

I missed the train, I said. I'm at Grand Central.

That Norman, she hissed. Put him on.

He's in the men's room.

What? I recognized the onset of hysteria in her voice. You have him call me the minute he's out. He's responsible for you, or has he forgotten? Well? I didn't answer. Listen, she said, her voice softening, I know it's not your fault. Just have him call me.

Okay.

I'll be waiting.

Sure, I said, and hung up.

Now I knew I'd be in trouble. I forgot, I would say. We went out for something to eat. I bought a pack of gum and a *Seventeen* magazine, then sat on a waiting room bench with the magazine close to my face. I only pretended to read; mostly I kept watch, peering over my magazine. I sat there alone, looking, not being looked at, waiting.

Bonita

He says, Quien? and we bow our heads, squinting into books. The room smells of Pine Sol, the room smells of baloney and socks. I've propped my book to shield my face. Across the aisle the boys sit, look-alike boys with Rugby shirts, wide white parts in their hair. We read about bullfights—Poetry!—says Señor Raul, agitating his slender hands. A turquoise on his pinkie, another in his ear, a shimmering shirt unbuttoned to the silver glint of a cross. In our book is a matador who could be Señor Raul.

Quien? he says, and I think, Me!

But he says, Maria, using fat Melinda's Spanish name. Fat Melinda, so dumb she cannot even conjugate ser.

No? Señor Raul clicks his tongue. I do not raise my hand.

After class girls huddle by the lockers. Giggling, gossiping, filing their nails, passing out gum to the circle. Girls in platforms, crepe-soled mules, rhinestone jeans, frosted eye shadow, clogs. Nice shoes, someone says. They all look at my brown Oxfords. Scuffed Oxfords from the Salvation Army, and they know that; we were seen leaving the store, our new clothes folded into paper bags, our mother dropping coins into her vinyl change purse.

The girls pop gum, smear on fruity gloss, tug at pleats, check makeup in compacts. The boys slam their lockers, belch for fun.

A compact snaps, a girl says, Here comes Betsy's boyfriend. Then his low voice behind me—Carmelita, mi amor. Does his hand on my shoulder leave a mark? He touches my hair, lifts a tangle to his nose. Bonita. I cannot look at him. The other girls do not speak.

His Period Six class has made piñatas—sombrero, burro, toro. They crowd the table, dangle from fluorescent lights. The boys swipe at them. Settle down, says Señor Raul. He plays a flamenco record, shows us some steps. We watch the way his hips move from side to side. The piñatas sway. I imagine one falling, breaking apart, candy spilling, Señor Raul slipping on the hard bright pieces, his eyes widening, looking to me for help. The record skips. Basta! says Señor Raul.

Wednesdays he has lunch duty. I sit on the girls' bench, my back to his pacing. But I can hear him whistling "Eres Tu," the scorched sugar and alcohol of his cologne another giveaway. The note he drops on my tray is folded in quarters. Carol Walsh grabs it and the other girls squeal, Read! Read! Carol Walsh, with her blonde veil, her fringe leather belt, her teeth that do not need braces. She stands up—a detention offense—flaps the note open and, Oooohhh it's so dirty! She flings the note onto my plate.

I wipe gravy from the yellow lined paper. In the bathroom stall, I will open it, afraid—What if it really is dirty? What if it's blank?— and see our linked initials inside a shaky heart.

I keep things. Acorns, shells, movie ticket stubs. Photos of my father squirreled from the family album and stored in a shoebox beneath my bed.

Señor Raul's notes, too, I keep in the box. Guapa and muchacha and amor. A touch leaves no mark, whispers vanish, but notes are real.

* * *

Miss Hormel blows her whistle and shouts Girls! Girls, we will not—repeat, not—flag. Counting, fifty, forty-nine.... The slap of our hands echoes through the gym. Girls making jumping jacks. Miss Hormel blows her whistle, crouches on gym-hardened legs, shouts, Go!

Girls in uniform, we do what we are told. My hands sting from slapping. Your bodies are machines, cries Miss Hormel. Twenty-two, twenty-one...We must maintain the machine.

Friday I spy him. We're coming out of Pantry Pride; his car, top down, is in the lot. Even if it wasn't the only red convertible in town—which it is—I'd know by the 007 plates. The car, thank God, is empty and I think, Please don't let him see us with our Pantry Pride bags and our dented old Ford and my grubby white shorts and my brother who hates everyone and my mother who is always either crying or saying your God damned father, but—Hey!—that's Señor Raul's car, my brother says, making kissing noises.

Who's Señor Raul? Why are you doing that? My mother shifts her weight, balancing bags, purse, keys.

I run to the back seat. Then I see him, coming from the liquor store. The woman he's with a barely grown-up version of Carol Walsh, her older sister maybe, if she has one. She touches his arm. He holds the car door. She twists the mirror to fix her lips. Bonita. Guapa. Amor. Does he call her this, whistling along with the radio, driving one-handed, the other hand...somewhere? I duck, my head resting on a four-pack of toilet paper.

Who the heck is Señor Raul? My mother won't stop.

Betsy's boyfriend. Well...ex.

Once on TV I saw a movie where the blonde actress rode in a convertible, whipping around the hills of France with the handsome leading man, her hair, her scarf waving. And that's how I see them, Señor Raul, this woman, flying down the Interstate, laughing, on their way to a movie or to eat at Egg Roll Palace.

* * *

In sewing class, we're making wrap-around skirts, reversible, which means you have to pay attention, you can't hide the mistakes inside. My mother has splurged on expensive material—striped silk, burgundy wool. So you won't be tempted to mess up, she says. Besides, it's about time they taught you something useful. Mrs. Winston actually smiled at the fabric. Her own clothes, she says, are all handmade.

We hunch over our machines, squint at thread, prick our fingers on pins, wind and unwind bobbins, mark seams with chalk. There are people—women—who do this all day. Mrs. Winston whacks a yardstick on the tables, she scissors the air, she holds up seams for ridicule. She holds up mine a lot. When she bends to inspect, her glasses bounce on their cord against her breasts.

Sewing is right after lunch, and he's slipped me another note, in the cafeteria line, near the desserts. I haven't read it yet.

Mrs. Winston is busy showing perfect Jenny Bradley how to make a perfect hem. I've finished my hem and there are only a few minutes until clean up, not enough time to start something new. I shouldn't do it, I know. I tell myself I won't. But Mrs. Winston is far across the room, busy with Jenny Bradley, who needs so much attention even though she's perfect and who gets it, never fail. They don't see me reach into my pocket, slip the folded note under my fabric, don't see me lift the edge, peek a word—Corazon!—then smooth the fabric flat. They don't see this, but Carol Walsh does, Carol Walsh who would be perfect as perfect Jenny Bradley if she could only learn to mind her own business which, of course, she cannot.

What's it say? she whispers. Pass it, pass it over!

Mrs. Winston looks. I know what she sees. Two girls who should be paying attention to their sewing, girls who need supervision, who need a good sharp whack of the yardstick to set them straight.

That hem! she cries, zooming in on my skirt from half a room away. That beautiful material and that...hem! Give it here! She snatches up my skirt, the note falls to the floor, and everyone stops sewing.

What is this? Mrs. Winston digs the glasses out of from between her breasts. Her face is a deflated ball. She unfolds the note, peers in disgust. In-deed! Does your mother know? We'll just put a stop to this. And she will, I know. The note goes into her desk drawer with the bobby pins, Rolaids, aspirin, thimbles and attendance book. I will never see it again. The bell will never ring.

Mrs. Winston waves her yardstick above her head. Clean up time, she announces. I take my spiked wheel, the one for marking patterns, and run it inside my palm then up and down my wrist where the veins are springy, pressing until it hurts. I imagine doing this to Mrs. Winston. The wheel is a buzz saw, I'm cutting her in half. Carol Walsh is next, then the other girls, Miss Hormel with her ropes and hoops and balance beam, runty Mr. Perry with his microscopes, and doughy Miss Lund. And the boys, all the boys, one by one they fall under my buzz saw. Then Señor Raul—him too—and my brother, my father, wherever he is, my mother and finally me, all of us severed.

With my seam ripper, I tear apart my hem. Mrs. Winston is right; it's a ragged hem, too ragged for such material. The stitches unravel. Once I start, I cannot stop. The side seams are harder, double-stitched, but I do it, I rip them, tearing the fabric with a noise that rouses Mrs. Winston from her desk. She shrieks—That fabric! Your skirt!—and comes running to me, shouting, You stupid girl, you willful, willful, stupid girl.

The Things That Claimed Her

She would come to think of those days as the time when she kept falling.

First it was a sidewalk crack. She was on her way home from the hospital. Indian summer, the sky enamel blue, a day she'd come to recall as nearly perfect. She was eating an apple, not paying attention, thinking about her mother, immobilized in bed, the room's low hum of machinery and the cabbagey smell of stacked dinner trays, then she was pitched forward, trying to right herself, the apple rolling from her hand onto the expensive-looking loafer.

You all right?

Can I help you?

He kicked the apple to the curb.

She was on the sidewalk. A man was offering his hand.

Let me help you, he said.

He eased her onto her feet. They really should do something about that sidewalk, he said. I've seen it happen before. His voice soothed away her embarrassment.

I'm fine, she said, but he kept his hand on her arm. Her knee was scraped, two of her fingernails broken. Nothing worse. Just a little shook up, she said. That's all.

Take a deep breath. It'll help.

That's when she looked at him. A tall man, solidly built. Dark hair, graying at the temples. A handsome man in loafers and jeans, a t-shirt beneath his wool blazer. He raised his eyebrows as if to say,

Isn't this amusing? The thing she felt then, all at once. A familiar feeling, lately submerged, a nascent sense of unease. She told herself no; she told herself stop. But when he suggested coffee—Just around the corner, I was on my way; it'll steady your nerves—she nodded and said yes.

At home her husband was stirring tomato sauce.

You're late, he said. How is she?

She opened the fridge, poured herself a glass of wine.

The same. We finished *Persuasion*. I mean, I did. I don't know what I'll read to her next. I keep telling myself she can hear me, but...

He gave the sauce a taste then switched on the burner beneath the pot of water. Since her mother's stroke he'd taken over the cooking—scrambled eggs, pasta with jarred sauce, tuna melts, comfort food that failed to comfort.

Angel hair tonight? Or do you want something heavier? Tortellini maybe?

She shrugged.

Sweetie, he said, moving in for a hug, I know it's hard. But she's, what? Eighty-two? And has had a good full life when you stop and think about it and...

She's not dead! Jesus, you talk like she's dead. She took a step backwards, out of his grasp. Besides, would it kill you to come with me once in a while?

He looked at her, blinking behind his glasses, as if wondering what he'd said wrong. In the two weeks since the stroke, he'd been to the hospital once. Hospitals, she knew, unnerved him. And to be fair he was overwhelmed, what with this being his tenure year, exams to grade, committee assignments, two conference presentations and an abstract still to finish, because if he were to succeed, if they were to stay here in this city they both loved, this city where she was born and where her mother (he did not say this) was now dying, and after all it would be different, wouldn't it, if her mother knew he was there but how could she possibly? This he really did say.

She went into the living room, set her glass on the windowsill. Across the street was another tall building, companion to their own, and for a moment she let her mind drift, imagining the lives taking place there. Families sitting down to dinner, mothers bathing small children, a woman putting on lipstick, a man straightening a tie. The wine was sharp and cold. She wanted another but did not want to return to the kitchen just yet. He hadn't meant anything. She knew that. About death he was simply matter of fact. His own parents had died in a car accident, years ago, when he was in high school; he'd been taken in by an aunt, also gone. And her father, she'd barely mourned his passing, that fleet presence in her life. Her mother, though. Always it had been the two of them. Holidays, birthdays, vacations. Summer trips to the shore. A series of cottages, sandy floors, her hair stiff with salt. Dancing in the kitchen to the polka show, her mother's large feet beneath her smaller ones. Afternoons keeping house while her mother worked, letting herself in with the spare key, heating whatever meal her mother had left to defrost, doing laundry, doing dishes and homework, studying hard, getting gold stars. My good girl, my gold star, her mother would say as the As piled up. You'll be the one, college girl, a big family and good job. I'm so proud of you.

Holidays, birthdays. Does she have to spend every single one with us, he'd asked at first. But how could they leave her alone? And eventually he'd come to accept, the dutiful son-in-law, smiling wanly, presiding over the table, then retreating into his study, his world of equations.

She felt hands on her shoulders, kneading. He'd brought in the bottle and he poured her another glass.

Dinner's ready, he said. Come eat.

* * *

She was rubbing lotion into her mother's hands, careful not to disturb the feeding tube or jiggle a vein. Veins wormy like the pulsing soil she and her mother would fill with tulip bulbs each fall. Her mother's skin was papery, her lips chapped. The lotion reeked of lilacs. She squeezed another dollop from the tube and moved her chair down the bed so she could smooth the cracked skin of her mother's feet. While she worked she made up stories, new ones every time. How much brighter, more animated her students seemed this year than last. How after a performance review, the principal had told her she'd be given a raise. How she, who rarely wore makeup, had stopped by Macy's for moisturizer and had been given a cosmetic bag full of samples: I put them aside for you. Her husband, he was being granted tenure. They were looking for a bigger place, one with a spare bedroom so she could stay over whenever she liked. And—guess what?—they were going to have a baby! Wasn't that great? Especially after how hard they'd been trying? That part, at least, was true. Except that recently they'd given up because what if he really didn't get tenure? They'd have to relocate. Or live on her schoolteacher's salary while he looked for other work. Better, he said, to wait and be certain because with two other people in the math department going up at the same time.... Besides, they were young still, barely forty.

Her mother stared. Impossible to tell what, if anything, she took in. Her hair—ash blonde, coiffed—was growing in coarse and gray. She would let no one brush it, grunting and snarling at any attempt. It would have to be cut. Before the stroke, her mother had been meticulous about her appearance. Earrings, perfume. Silk scarf at her throat. Tubes of rouge, lipstick, a touch of eye shadow, flick of powder. A little makeup never hurt, she'd say, snapping her compact shut.

Boy or girl, I don't care, so long as it's healthy.

On the other side of the curtain that separated the room's two beds, a woman was snoring, a woman she'd never seen. As far as she could tell, the woman had no visitors.

We were so excited, we drank champagne to celebrate. I know I'm not supposed to drink in my condition, but one teeny little glass, what harm could it do?

She put the cap back on the lotion and returned the tube to her mother's bedside drawer.

For an hour or so her husband had stopped by, fidgeting in his visitor's chair. She would stay until the doctor came, she told him, then have dinner with a friend. And if he didn't ask which friend, did she need to say?

At the bar they drank champagne. Just one she vowed. A way to unwind after such a day. He was telling a funny story, one about a Halloween party the year before. He'd gone as Cyrano de Bergerac but—wouldn't you know it?—someone else came as the same damned thing. What were the odds? Although, he said, I believe I had the natural advantage, and he'd touched his nose, his fine Roman nose, how regal he looked, an emperor, one of the benign ones. Smiling, yes, but something grave in his expression too. She felt loose-limbed, elastic.

Overhead the TV was set to a football game. Padded, helmeted men piled on top of each other, spilling onto the too bright grass. She knew nothing about football. For a while her husband had tried explaining the game to her and for his sake she'd feigned interest until, exasperated by her lack of comprehension, her confusion over scoring and penalties, he'd given up.

They ordered refills, small plates of food to share.

He told her about his job as an urban planner. How entire neighborhoods could change, small businesses and apartment complexes springing up where nothing had been before, nothing but empty lots. He worked here in the city mostly, though there were occasional out of town jobs. Did she, herself, get away much?

Not much, she confessed. A trip to Spain, years earlier. Some long weekends upstate. You know how it is.

He did. He had been married divorced married divorced. Fool me once, shame on you, he said. Fool me twice... well, I guess that makes me the fool. The way he laughed, she felt lighter somehow. She had told him she was married, of course. She made references, my husband this-or-that. And there was her ring. About her mother she could not bear to speak.

Small plates of food piled up, one after another, and she ate until she felt sated.

In the ladies' room she checked her phone—no messages. She reapplied lipstick, smoothed her hair.

Outside, before she could hail a cab, he said, I want to kiss you. She was startled, uncertain what to say. He touched her hair. She turned up her collar against the nip in the air and, in a gesture that surprised her, she turned up his collar, too. Then they were kissing beneath the jaundiced light of a streetlamp, kissing long and hard as if they were teenagers with nowhere to go. It felt silly, she thought, to be kissing like this in public at her age. And then she stopped thinking altogether.

In the taxi home she sucked on a breath mint. She pulled her hair into a bun, wiped her lipstick on her exposed wrist and rubbed in the stain.

The taxi pulled away just a little too quickly, and she stumbled on the curb, nearly falling, righting herself just in time.

They would paint the nursery yellow, a nice neutral color because, she explained, she did not want to know what to expect. She needed things. Stroller, cradle, bottles. She rattled off names. What did her mother think about this one or that? Earlier that day the doctor had said it was simply a matter of time. She'd repeated the phrase to herself—a matter of time—nothing simple about it.

But suppose he was wrong? Suppose she rallied? Stranger things had been known to occur. She might open her eyes, say Yes, Michael,

Grace, those are lovely names, and what, by the way, am I doing in this bed? And then? Erase the lies with new ones? A miscarriage—no need to look for a larger place. It was common enough. She touched her stomach, the taut muscles there.

The woman on the other side of the curtain was coughing, a rattle deep within her chest. Soon visiting hours would be over. She had lessons to plan, stacks of spelling quizzes to grade. *Spell school, house, dinner. Spell mother, nursery. Spell hospital, seizure, Do Not Resuscitate.* Her eyelids felt heavy. Softly she hummed the songs she knew her mother loved, songs from musicals they'd seen ages ago. Edelweiss. Sunrise, Sunset. Happy songs when she could think of them. Wash That Man Right Out of My Hair.

Her husband had left a pile of books on the living room floor. She'd nearly tripped over it. What the hell? she'd screamed. Can't you once, just once, pick up after yourself?

Unfair, she knew. He'd taken the books into his study and shut the door.

In bed that night he held her and said, I know.

What, she wanted to ask him, what is it that you think you know?

Afternoon sun streamed through his bedroom window, lighting up the parquet, striping the bare walls. He cradled her, mumbled words into her hair: *Bella. Mi amore.* She answered in her high school French: *Tu est beau; je t'adore.* Foreign phrases divorced from any real meaning, light as air.

The room was chilly and she squirmed down into the blankets, resting her head on his chest so that his voice sounded hollow. She felt wonder at his presence in her life, wonder that she should be there, in his bed, that she should lie so easily, no need to say anything, really, since her husband rarely asked much. Far below them buses rumbled, car horns blared, so many people rushing about, headed somewhere. She was thirsty. Soon he would be gone, six months at least, an urban renewal project on the west coast. For this, too, he had a language: mixed use development, empowerment zone, revitalize the urban core, his words a small pile of stones between them. Whenever he spoke this way she tried to pay attention, but before she could help it her mind would wander to her mother. She should tell him, she knew. Only sometimes, during the closest moments, those moments when there was no need to talk, a sweetness took over, one she did not wish to spoil with words, a sweetness that lasted until he said something or she looked at the clock or someone's phone rang and all at once they returned, all the things that claimed her, doctors and waivers, powers of attorney, health proxy, medical bills, papers piling up, demanding her life, all of it. She would go home then to her plate of pasta or eggs, her husband's eyes red with fatigue, the two of them falling into fitful sleep, exhausted for their different reasons.

He was saying something now, something about getting away. Soon, before he had to leave. Her husband would be out of town, a conference, she'd told him that much. A quick trip to the country, perhaps. They'd drive around, look at foliage, go on a hike. Could she manage it?

She should tell him, she knew, but she could not.

I can't, she said.

No? Well of course, if you're too busy… He sat up, reached for his cigarettes. You don't have to decide now. A day trip maybe. We'll rent some bikes…

I can't ride a bike. It was true, but it was not what she had meant to say.

What? Impossible! Everyone can ride a bike. He blew a long stream of smoke towards the window and she watched it dissipate. I'll teach you.

* * *

She was singing, barely audible, some half-remembered child-hood tune, nonsense words because she was at a loss for things to say. Their time together had not been easy. A late life baby from a mid-life affair, she was the daughter of a woman who had always been old. Her mother's eyes were mica chips, her forehead furrowed and dry. She made a guttural sound, then another and another in quick succession. She was…humming. Her mother was humming the song. Her expression had softened and though she could not smile, something had changed within her, lighting her face. They hummed the song together and when they finished her mother shut her eyes.

On the Saturday her husband was away they rented a bike and wheeled it into the park, to a brown patch of lawn ringed by benches. Teenaged boys in hoodies sat, legs splayed, dragging on cigarettes, nothing to do. An old man in an overcoat drank from a paper bag. A scabby black mutt, seemingly ownerless, dug a hole beneath a tree then covered it up.

In the rental shop he'd examined several models, looking for something basic, choosing at last a three speed, low to the ground, in a reassuring shade of pastel blue. At his insistence she wore a helmet.

She was dubious about the lesson, afraid of falling. Whenever she'd tried before she'd quickly lost her balance, her *equilibrium.* You have to maintain your equilibrium, her mother had said, as if that were in her control. Again and again she would topple, until she told herself she didn't care, riding a bike was a stupid pastime, dangerous even. And now she was trusting this man, this near stranger, because…why? She'd refused to go away with him, refused to give a reason. Yet here he was. And in less than a week he would be leaving, no question of her accompanying him.

He wheeled the bike to a place where the ground leveled out. Dead leaves crunched underfoot. He had promised to catch her; he would not let her fall. He lowered the kickstand and she mounted, feeling giddy, the ground miles away. She practiced pedaling; he showed her how to brake. Ready? he said. He grabbed the handlebars and kicked the kickstand free. The bike wobbled beneath her but he kept hold of the handlebars, walking backwards to steady her. Great he said. You're doing great! Without warning he let go. For a moment, a brief, exhilarating moment, she stayed upright, peddling madly, amazing how buoyant she felt, the bike steady then veering, hitting something—a rock, a bump—so that she was in free-fall, careening sideways, pulling the bike down with her, onto him, his arm bent behind his head, a grimace contorting his face.

It was she who helped him up. She who wheeled the bike back, who hailed a taxi and waited in the emergency room while they x-rayed and plastered his broken arm, she who paid the cab fare home, who poured strong whiskeys and brought them to where he lay propped in bed then fed him Chinese take out, noodles spilling from her chopsticks onto the sheet. She would stay all night. In the morning she would leave for the hospital after telling him where she was going and why. She knew this. But for now she let him rest.

Years later, when they recounted how they met, they would laugh about this day, this *mishap* as he liked to call it, the time he promised to catch her and had broken her fall, a thing that never ceased to astonish her.

Accident

She bounces Baby on a flowery hip, kisses his fist, uncurling slug fingers from pearls. She dances him, coos and coos. Baby rides her hip. Big birthin' hips, that's what Sir said, and slapped her behind. She was big then.

Her dress has red flowers, but brides wear white. The bride on the cake has white flowers and the groom has a long black coat. When she sliced the first slice, Sir smashed it into her mouth, smearing frosting. She licked her lips and laughed. I drank a drink that fizzed in my nose. You see? she told Aunt Alice and snatched it away. See how I always have to watch? Aunt Alice held Baby, he squirmed and cried. I cannot hold him. Not one of your dolls, Sir says, and boys should not play with dolls.

The music changes from slow to fast. Oops! she cries and hoists Baby over her head. His little legs kick. He is a fish, fish can swim. My cousins dance with each other, Heather and Rose, they are girls. They do the curtsey, the spin, they make their skirts twirl so I can see the lace of their petticoats.

Under the tent it is hot. The ladies wear sleeveless and the men have their jackets on the backs of folding chairs. My new shirt is scratchy, my trousers have pleats. My hair is short, they will cut it shorter.

People dance under the tent, sway to the tapes that Sir plays in his truck, songs about when times get tough. Brutus howls, wanting out. But she will not have him in the yard, not on this day, not even chained to his house. The only time she's let him in because she is afraid of him, makes him stay in the yard with the shed for Sir's tools and the two cars on cinder blocks and her garden of tomatoes, still green. But it's better than before, she says, even with him howling that racket, better than those two small rooms, you on the couch, admit. Because at least you have your own room now and can go play in the yard.

Brutus lives in the yard.

Today he's locked in my room but he cannot go in my bed. He can go in Baby's crib, chew the rails off Baby's crib, he can chew on dirty old diapers from the dirty old diaper pail. He cannot go in my bed with the thumbtacks I put there or sit on my chair that I turned upside-down or climb on my desk.

Let him try. I hope.

Aunt Alice comes to my table, brings me milk, another slice of cake. Drink it, she says, fanning herself with a folded paper plate. The breeze she makes feels good on my neck. But the milk is warm and I do not want milk. I take pretend sips, smooth the holes in the frosting where the bride was stuck in. Or maybe the groom.

Sir is the groom, the husband now, and he wears a suit not a long black coat, not those greasy overalls and dusty boots and the oil on his fingernails from the carburetors and transmissions and all the things he talks about.

I will not say his name.

When Aunt Alice leaves, when no one is looking, I dump the milk under the table, watch it pool on the grass. That other time was an accident. She was big then and slipped on the puddle on the living room floor and the baby came, too fast. That is why, I know, why they're sending me. But it was an accident.

Accident: Not on purpose.

Boys do not spill milk they do not play with dolls. They do not cry just because they are going away.

Eugene, it's a stupid name.

I did not want to leave her in the hospital. I did not want to go with Sir. She was in bed with Baby brand new and the nurse said big boy like you, carrying on, aren't you ashamed?

At home Sir said lucky for you. He said we'll have no more of your antics, you'll see. Now she has a baby to look after. They put the crib in my room but said do not touch. Baby cries at night and crying is for babies.

The song ends, goes back to slow. My cousins come over with Heather's new doll. It has long red hair and a candy name. Melanie. Melony. Vanilla lemony caramel Melanie, I like that name. Rose's doll we call Ugly Linda because of the scratches on her face and the way her eye is pulled out. I didn't do it though.

The day they gave Baby a name they showed me a brochure. Boys in t-shirts doing push-ups. Little men, she said. Little men like you. The brochure had other photos—boys saluting, boys aiming rifles, boys at a long table, their heads bowed.

They took Baby to church and the priest said his name and splashed him with water. He chanted words I did not know, a spell for Baby, a spell with water. The bowl was high on a stand. I stood on tip-toe to reach it, I splashed my face. Special water for Baby. Sir grabbed my wrist and said something that made the priest stop. He crossed himself, said our father, but I said he's not. Sir is not my father my father is the one whose car went off the road two icy days after I was born. I have his photo. Look she told me. Your eyes. Your mouth. The spitting image. She kept the photo in the album and we'd sit side by side on the couch with the album spread across both our laps and the lamp low and the cabbagey smell coming from the kitchen and the heat banging in the pipes. Now the photo is in my suitcase.

It's better you'll see, she said on the ride home. One hundred miles we'll drive back and forth all the time before you know it you won't even miss us.

Sir had other words. Discipline, behavior. Separate the men from. Great big Mama's boy, learn to toughen up, until she told him Eugene hush and for once he really did.

Soon they will say when. My suitcase is under the bed where Brutus can go, where I put his rawhide bone. They will say when, load the suitcase in Sir's truck and drop me.

Heather says here, hold Melanie. She wants to be a bride, wants to catch the bouquet, it is time, the ladies lining up, bumping each other. My mother passes Baby to Sir. But instead of tossing her flowers, she walks over to me, arms open wide, smiling, perfumey, lips so red. Let's dance she says and she is beautiful more beautiful than Melanie or any doll I can imagine and while we are dancing there is nothing for anyone to do but watch.

Sunrise

She turns in bed, too early to rise, the sky sickly yellow, red-rimmed. *Red in the morning, sailors take warning.* But she is not adrift, mattress firm beneath her, box springs, bed frame, concrete floor. She has risen too early is all, tossing and turning through a sleepless night, no particular reason, the occasional mild disturbance she attributes to age. The sun has not yet risen, curious phrase, the sun as we know neither rising nor setting, fixed in the sky, unmoving, planets spinning around it, turning and turning on their axes. She does not feel this, of course, the earth's rotation; such a thing would be intolerable, the unceasing sensation of movement, the constant reminder of time.

The day has not taken a turn for the worse, figure of speech, but still. The phone has not rung, she has no premonition, no reason to be awake so early in the morning, a Sunday, the second in May, the one with flowers and cards.

She lies still. She thinks of her son.

He would be driving now, moving back home, another year of college completed, exams taken, courses passed. She is moved by the thought of this, the long drive East, suitcases in the well, music playing, sun in his eyes. Miles to go. He would have left early, the sky barely light. Would drive for hours, passing borders, towns then states. Too soon yet to turn off the highway, too soon to stop for coffee, for gas, a quick pee—*Hey, your lights are on!*—thanking the attendant, looking away just long enough to do that, to switch them off, not seeing the driver, the other car running a light, looking up too late, blinded by the sun.

In bed, the woman tosses and turns. Morning has not yet begun; she knows she should sleep but the thought of him, alone on the still dark road, causes something to rise in her, some feeling she must quell. Her fears inchoate, not concrete, she cannot put a name to them. Sleep is all, sleep is what she needs.

She turns on the light.

Soon he will be here, the phone has not rung, and though she cannot feel it, the earth is still moving, no way to make this moment stop, though later, sooner than she can know, that is all she will want.

Previously Published Stories

Grateful acknowledgement to the editors at the following literary journals where these stories first appeared, sometimes in slightly different form:

"Wakey Nights" in *Shenandoah*

"Sea Change," "Luck Was A Taxi," and "Sunrise" in *Confrontation*

"But Now Am Found" in *Bellevue Literary Review*

"Never Let Go" in *Georgetown Review*

"Griswold" in *descant*

"To The Stranger Who Brings Flowers" in *Dappled Things*

"Vigil" in *Iron Horse Literary Review*

"Poinsettias" in *Saranac Review*

"Hold On Fast" in *The Laurel Review*

"In My Solitude" (as "Flesh") in *iris*

"Bonita" in *Puerto del Sol*

"Accident" in *580 Split*

Acknowledgments

Many thanks to Diane Goettel and the wonderful staff at Black Lawrence Press for believing in this book and shepherding it through production.

For the gift of time and financial support I wish to thank Framingham State University and The New York Foundation for the Arts.

For providing me with a beautiful space in which to work, thanks to Carey Shea, Calvin Parker, Mike Rafa, and Kristen Hoft.

For his visual acumen and patience thank you to Christopher DeLuca.

For myriad kindnesses thank you to Randy Bailey, Agnes Criss, Robert Dow, Lisa Eck, Elizabeth Fairfield, Jodie Fink, Lisa Gaughran, Marita Golden, Mia Herman, Michelle Hoover, Howard Horvath Sr. and. Jr., Susan Jaafar, Lousie Kirstel, Jane Rosenberg LaForge, Maryellen Latas, Joseph G. Lurio, Carlos Mayol, Desmond McCarthy, Martha McPhee, Mike McTigue, Lisa Merrill, Cheryl Mwaria, Jay Neugeboren, Cindy Rosenthal, Ralph Saunders, Rolf Semprebon, Kate Southwood, Susan Steinberg, Michelle Valois, Sam Witt, and my mother, Maureen Cotter.

Above all to my late husband, Jeffrey LeBlanc, for twenty years of love and encouragement, humor and support.

Photo: Carol Rosegg

Patricia Horvath is the author of the memoir *All the Difference* (Etruscan Press). Her stories and essays have been published widely in literary journals including *The Massachusetts Review, The Los Angeles Review, Confrontation,* and *Shenandoah.* She is the recipient of New York Foundation for the Arts Fellowships in both fiction and literary nonfiction, the Goldenberg Prize for Fiction at *Bellevue Literary Review,* and the Frank O'Connor Award for Fiction at *descant.* She teaches at Framingham State University. Her website is https://patricialhorvath.com/.